I0822544

Ghost Canyon

A Fernando Lopez Santa Fe Mystery

Also by James C. Wilson from Sunstone Press:

Hiking New Mexico's Chaco Canyon: The Trails, The Ruins, The History

The Fernando Lopez Santa Fe Mystery Series

Peyote Wolf
Smokescreen

Ghost Canyon

A Fernando Lopez Santa Fe Mystery

JAMES C. WILSON

SANTA FE

Sunstone books may be purchased for educational, business, or sales promotional use. For information please write: Special Markets Department, Sunstone Press, P.O. Box 2321, Santa Fe, New Mexico 87504-2321.

Design › R. Ahl

ISBN 9781632934079 (hardcover)

eBook 978-1-61139-646-1

Library of Congress Cataloging-in-Publication Data

Names: Wilson, James C., 1948- author. | Wilson, James C., 1948- Fernando Lopez Santa Fe mystery.
Title: Ghost Canyon / James C. Wilson.
Description: Santa Fe, New Mexico : Sunstone Press, [2021] | Series: A Fernando Lopez Santa Fe mystery | Summary: "When a park ranger is murdered at Chaco Culture National Historical Park in New Mexico, Santa Fe Police Detective Fernando Lopez and FBI Agent Patricia Begay must navigate a 1,200-year-old landscape of ghosts and ruins to find the murderer and expose a ring of looters trafficking in ancient tribal artifacts"-- Provided by publisher.
Identifiers: LCCN 2021048256 | ISBN 9781632933522 (paperback) | ISBN 9781611396461 (epub) | ISBN 1632933527 (paperback)
Subjects: LCSH: Lopez, Fernando (Fictitious character) | Murder--Investigation--Fiction. | Archaeological thefts--New Mexico--Fiction. | LCGFT: Detective and mystery fiction.
Classification: LCC PS3623.I58485 G48 2021 | DDC 813/.6--dc23/eng/20211013
LC record available at https://lccn.loc.gov/2021048256

WWW.SUNSTONEPRESS.COM
SUNSTONE PRESS / POST OFFICE BOX 2321 / SANTA FE, NM 87504-2321 /USA
(505) 988-4418

Dedicated to the ancient Chacoans for their genius and their magic.

PREFACE

I have been hiking and camping in Chaco Canyon for nearly fifty years. During this time the canyon has changed radically. When I first started visiting, back in the mid-seventies, you came into the canyon on the old Highway 57, plunging over the lip of the canyon and careening down a rutted dirt road to Casa Chiquita, a small Great House on the West Mesa Trail.

Once in the canyon you could drive and hike virtually anywhere you wanted. You rarely encountered other visitors on the lonely trails, only the ruins of the 1,200-year-old city littered with Chaco Black-on-White pottery shards. And there was something else: the feeling that you were not alone. You could feel the presence of the ancient ones in a way that I had never experienced before or after those early years.

I remember one memorable camping trip to Chaco. We were sitting at our campfire when a park ranger came over and began regaling us with ghost stories.

The ranger told us about hearing strange noises that sounded like chanting or singing, and about seeing mysterious lights and fires around the ruins. The ranger offered no explanations for the mysteries they had encountered. Back then I didn't know quite what to think about the ghost stories. Still don't, so I will quote my detective in Ghost Canyon:

"He neither believed nor dis-believed in ghosts, but he'd lived in magical Santa Fe long enough to know there were more things in this life than could be explained by a simple rationalist philosophy. That was especially true in places like Santa Fe and Chaco Canyon, where cultures and entire civilizations were layered on top of each other, haunting each other. You couldn't walk—or dig—anywhere in this state without uncovering bones and artifacts of the ancient ones. All New Mexicans walked on haunted ground."

So where better to set a mystery than Chaco Canyon?

Shadows in the Ruins

Pete Chavez waited until the last streaks of crimson faded from the western sky. The canyon plunged into darkness as he left the visitor center and walked to the staff jeep parked outside. He'd been assigned to do the evening security check and lock-up this week, a duty the rangers rotated weekly. One of them had to lock the gate every evening at sunset and drive around the eight-mile Chaco loop to make sure everyone was out of the park. Leaving it open at night would invite looters, night photographers and others who could engage in nefarious activity that would damage the fragile, 1200-year-old ruins. Opening at seven in the morning and closing at sunset kept visitors on the straight and narrow–most of the time.

Pete climbed into the jeep and hit the ignition and then the lights. Their twin beams revealed the hulking shadow of North Mesa straight ahead. He drove around the short curve to the metal gate and jumped out of the jeep. Locking the gate behind him, he noticed a three-quarter moon rising over Chacra Mesa at the east end of the canyon. Back on the road, he drove off slowly into the darkness. On the other side of the one-way Chaco Loop he saw a last vehicle approaching the exit gate, which he would close and lock on his way out.

Other than his jeep and the other vehicle, not a single light shone in the dark canyon. The twin beams of his headlights revealed the empty asphalt ahead. He always drove slowly at night to avoid the deer and elk herds that lived in the canyon and came down from the mesas to feed in the wash at night. He prided himself on never having hit any of the magnificent animals, something he couldn't say about a couple of the other rangers.

So when he saw the black object in his headlights he had plenty of time to apply his brake. Slowing down, he approached what turned out to be a large buck elk with seven or eight point antlers and mottled fur, indicating it had not totally shed its winter coat. The animal seemed confused, moving forward and backward and then turning in a circle as if it had lost its inner compass. He stopped the jeep and was about to get out when the elk lowered its head and charged.

The animal's antlers struck the driver's side of the jeep as Pete recoiled from the door. The crazed animal bounced off the jeep and then disappeared into the saltbush along the road. Vanished.

Shaken, he put the jeep in gear and drove off down the road. Did the animal have rabies? How else explain its erratic behavior?

He drove even slower now, afraid of what he might encounter next. Past the Hungo Pavi and Chetro Ketl ruins, their crumbling stone walls now illuminated by the moonlight. Only the empty doorways and windows remained pitch black, concealing their dark interiors. The windows especially looked like gigantic eyes watching him from afar.

Now he approached the massive Pueblo Bonito ruin, a 650-room Great House built at the foot of North Mesa. Usually he bypassed the parking lot and continued on around the Chaco Loop. Tonight he pulled into the Bonito parking lot and stopped, still disturbed by his encounter with the elk. He turned off the engine and sat thinking in the open jeep, trying to decide whether he should report the incident to county animal control.

Suddenly lights flickered behind Pueblo Bonito. Or was he imagining them? Spooked now, he grabbed his flashlight and climbed out of the jeep. They hadn't encountered any night hikers or photographers in months. He didn't want to think about the other possibility: that someone could be digging illegally, searching for ancient pots or jewelry. Looting.

Unfortunately, his flashlight batteries were weak. He kept shaking the flashlight to keep the light on as he walked down the trail to Pueblo Bonito. He saw the light again, more of a glow now. It seemed to be coming from the northwest corner of the Great House, near the base of North Mesa. He decided against going around behind Bonito because it was shaded from the moonlight and too dark. Instead, he walked up to the south wall and switched off his flashlight.

He waited a moment to give his eyes time to adjust to the semi-darkness and then stepped through an ancient doorway into an open plaza. Blocks of rooms surrounded the plaza in a semicircle, their jagged walls casting grotesque shadows on the white sand of the plaza. He crept along the north-south wall into the heart of the ruin. As he moved into the shadows he heard what sounded like a shovel or pickaxe striking stone. Now he was certain looters were digging in the ruin. He paused for a moment, considering whether to return to the visitor center for reinforcements. The looters could be armed and dangerous.

Suddenly the light ahead went out and the digging stopped. They had noticed his presence. It was too late to go back.

He held the flashlight tightly, his only weapon. With his left hand out in front and his right hand holding the flashlight he crept forward toward where he had heard the noise. He came to a stairway down into a block of connected rooms. Feeling with his foot, he moved down the stairway step by step. He sensed movement in the room but resisted turning on his flashlight.

Just as he reached the bottom a flash of light illuminated the room. Blinded, he covered his eyes momentarily. When he opened them he saw a shadow, what looked like a black figure coming out of the light. He wore a long black duster and a wide-brimmed hat and seemed to float across the room toward him, reaching out a hand now, trying to communicate.

He shrank back, away from the probing hand.

Suddenly he lost his balance and stumbled backward. Then out of the corner of his eye he saw the flash of an object. The blow to the side of his head pitched him forward into darkness.

Part One: Santa Fe

1

Detective Fernando Lopez of the Santa Fe Police Department sat at his small corner table at the Shed, his favorite restaurant. He'd come over for a quick lunch and to get away from all the people with problems. As always he'd asked for this one-person table pushed up against the window. Here he didn't have to look at the tourists who gathered at the larger tables behind him. Too damn many tourists in Santa Fe these days. You had to arrive by eleven o'clock for lunch if you didn't want to wait in line for hours outside on the patio. The damn tourists had ruined the only place where you could get real New Mexican food in downtown Santa Fe.

He'd just finished eating his mocha cake dessert when his cellphone rang. "Fernando, this is your lucky day," said Linda Stephens, the police dispatcher. "Chief wants you to check out a homicide on East Alameda. Housekeeper found the body this morning. Forensics is already there."

"Lucky me," he said, leaving a twenty dollar bill on the table and walking out of the restaurant. The throng of tourists waiting on the patio parted to allow him to pass. He turned the corner and walked down the block to the Washington Avenue station.

Once inside he stood at the front counter while Linda shuffled through a stack of papers mumbling to herself.

He loved Linda's sense of humor. An old hippie with long gray hair and a wicked sense of humor, she'd moved down to Santa Fe from Taos in the late 1970s after becoming disillusioned with living in the New Buffalo commune. He'd had a brief affair with Linda many years ago, his only indiscretion in the forty years he'd been married to Estelle. They'd broken it off to save their friendship...as well as his marriage.

"Who's the victim?"

"Tom Flynn. You know, that old eccentric guy you sometimes see on the Plaza selling art, or the crappy little paintings he calls art."

He nodded. "I know who you mean."

"Here's the address." She handed him a slip of paper.

The address surprised him. Upscale East Alameda happened to be one of the quietest neighborhoods in Santa Fe.

Outside, he took his old Plymouth Acclaim out of the parking lot and drove up to the Paseo and around to the address he was given on East Alameda Street. He crossed the bridge over the Santa Fe River, bone dry as it usually was in early June, before the onset of the monsoon season in July.

He pulled in behind the cruiser and police van already in the driveway and looked around at the old adobe house and the patch of cactus out front, a tangled mess of overgrown prickly pear and cholla stalks. The house looked like one of the original bungalows from the 1920s, similar to his little adobe on Acequia Madre, except this one was badly in need of repair: a fresh coat of stucco, new windows and door, and especially a new roof. He saw where a blue plastic tarp had been placed on the roof near the front door. Not a good sign.

Sergeant Antonio Blake was waiting for him on the porch. A big burly ex-Marine with hands as big as a catcher's mitt, Antonio nodded as he approached.

"Miguel and Teresa are almost finished. We kept the housekeeper here figuring you'd want to talk to her. Maria Lujan's her name. She's on the back patio waiting for you. There's also a guy in the guesthouse, an old drunk who looks and talks like a derelict. We're not sure if he was a friend of Tom Flynn's or Flynn's renter. He's indisposed at the moment, if you know what I mean."

He did not know what Antonio meant, but he stepped inside the little adobe, which smelled strongly of decomposing flesh. He found himself looking at a clutter of ancient Navajo rugs, clunky Mexican furniture and bookshelves stacked with dusty kachinas, Pueblo pottery, and assorted knick-knacks collected over a lifetime in Santa Fe. Stacks of magazines and newspapers littered the floor. Empty vodka bottles spilled over the coffee table onto the rug. Whoever lived here was clearly an alcoholic—and dysfunctional.

In the arched doorway to a back bedroom he saw the body of Tom Flynn sprawled out on the floor. A tiny wisp of a man who in death looked more like a mummy drug out of some ancient tomb and tossed on the floor, a bag of bones wrapped in cloth. Long white hair matted with dried blood, arms and legs as thin as pencils, wearing filthy plaid pajamas and bedroom slippers. His face was bloody and disfigured, and his head was turned to the side and twisted back at a 45-degree angle.

Whoever killed him had pounded his face and then snapped his neck like a dry twig.

"How long has he been dead?" Fernando asked, pulling a handkerchief out of his pocket and covering his nose and mouth.

"We think he's been dead a couple of days," Teresa said. "Looks like his neck was broken. Lots of facial trauma. Not a pretty sight."

He noticed a metal cane off to one side of the body. He saw dried blood on the end. "Looks like he put up a fight."

"Lotta good it did him."

Stepping over the body, he entered a bedroom as dark and pungent as a dungeon with heavy curtains and a drawn shade over the one lone window. He stumbled over a cardboard box overflowing with paper on his way to the window, where he quickly raised the shade and threw open the curtains to let some light into the dark room.

What he saw puzzled him. The floor was littered with ancient yellowed papers and notebooks that looked like some damn library archive. As best he could figure, someone had taken the cardboard box and angrily thrown its contents onto the floor in one angry motion. Looking for something. And in a big hurry.

"What's this?"

Antonio followed him into the room. "It's a box of old family photos and papers, genealogies, that sort of thing. Flynn was from an old Santa Fe family. I guess he saved all their documents."

Fernando pushed the papers around on the floor with his foot, seeing nothing of interest. So he went to the closet and looked though the clothing, blankets, and piles of shoes. Again, nothing caught his attention.

"Take a look at this." Antonio pointed to a leather-bound book open on the unmade bed.

He walked over and studied the book. "Go tell Miguel and Teresa to bag this before they leave. It might have been what the perpetrator was looking for. Look, a page has been ripped out."

"Yeah, but it could have been ripped out long ago."

"I don't think so," Fernando said. "Look at the torn paper hanging from the binding."

While Antonio went to tell forensics, he put on a pair of latex gloves and picked up the leather volume. The book turned out to be a journal kept by one Alton Flynn, who he assumed was Tom Flynn's grandfather since the journal began in the 1890s and ended in 1910. Someone had torn out a single page and left the rest of the book. It seemed highly unlikely that someone would kill Tom Flynn just to get a page from a hundred-year-old journal, but he wanted to take a closer look when he had the time.

He waited until forensics came, making sure they bagged the journal. Then he wandered into the next room, a studio with a row of east-facing windows and slightly better light. He walked across an old gray linoleum floor splattered with paint of every color in the rainbow to a wooden easel propped up against the wall.

On the easel were miniature paintings of dogs, chickens, horses, and other animals, all done with thick splotches of oil paint on plywood, mostly yellows, reds, and blues. In fact, they were all composed of yellows, reds, and blues, as if Tom Flynn had run out of any other colors. They looked like the kind of work done in an elementary school art class. Crude but cute, if you were fond of bright splotchy animals made out of plywood.

He did remember seeing Tom Flynn on the Plaza harassing tourists, begging them to buy one of his miniatures. He called them 'Animal Crackers.' Not exactly the kind of art tourists in up-scale Santa Fe were looking to purchase and take back to their palatial abodes.

Finally he stepped out of the rear door and found the housekeeper on a flagstone patio. She was sitting by herself on a crude wooden bench that at one time had been yellow with red and blue chickens painted on its sides. She sat quietly with her hands in her lap, a small woman in her mid to late fifties wearing jeans, a long gray sweater, and a bandana wrapped around her head. She looked uncomfortable, and nervous.

He introduced himself. "So you're the housekeeper?"

"No, Mr. Tom no keep house." She laughed. "I come over to cook for him two or three times a week. He give me a key, because sometimes he can't come to the door, you know. He drinks a lot. I found him this morning when I came in about ten o'clock. That's when I called police."

"Have you seen anyone else in the house this week, say during the last two or three days?"

"No, Mr. Tom don't have many friends," she said solemnly. "He's not a nice man when he drinks, you know. He gets angry and says things. Sometimes he don't pay me for my work, I don't know why. He gets angry is all. The only person I see here recently was Mr. Clint, who lives in the little house. He comes over so they can drink together mostly. I cook for him too, but he's not a nice man either when he drinks. I'm afraid of Mr. Clint."

"Why, has Mr. Clint threatened you?" he asked.

She avoided his eyes. "No, only when he drinks. They drink too much, you know. Get crazy like that."

While they spoke, a young man holding a cell phone walked around the side of the house into the back yard. He seemed to be in a hurry. Agitated. "Hey—are you coming?" he yelled at Maria Lujan.

She blushed. "My son, Luis."

"Let's go! I have to be somewhere!" He stopped when he saw Fernando. "What do you want with my mother?"

"Detective Fernando Lopez, Santa Fe Police," he introduced himself. "We're investigating a homicide here. What can I do for you?'

The kid changed his attitude instantly. "Oh, sorry...I'm here to pick up my mother."

He turned to Maria and handed her a business card. "If you think of anything else, anything that might help, give me a call."

She tucked the card into her purse.

Then he noticed the gash on the young man's forehead, a fresh wound. The kind of wound a cane might make if it struck a man's forehead in an act of self-defense. Or anger.

"What happened to your forehead?"

"It's nothing, just an accident." With that the young man turned and walked away talking on his cellphone. His mother followed tentatively, glancing back at him.

He watched as the two of them walked away, the son still talking on his cellphone and the mother trying to keep up as they made their way through a tangle of weeds back to the front of the house.

He didn't have time to dwell on the Lujans. Right now he needed to find out more about this Clint character who lived in Tom Flynn's guesthouse and who intimidated Maria Lujan. A drunk and a derelict, according to Antonio.

The guesthouse was about two hundred feet from the back patio, halfway up the ridge to Canyon Road. The tiny structure looked in even worse condition than the big house, with rusted casement windows and huge cracks in the stucco. The gravel path to the porch was overgrown with weeds. The front door was ajar and difficult to budge when he tried to give it a push.

"Anybody home?" he asked, shoving against the door with all his weight until the door swung inward, scraping against the floorboards.

As soon as he stepped inside he saw why nobody had responded.

The two-room guesthouse reeked of garbage and soiled linen, with dirty dishes and empty vodka bottles stacked high in the kitchen area. Discarded clothing and blankets were draped over the Taos Sofa and leather chair in the living room. Stacks of cheap paperbacks and yellowed newspapers cluttered the floor, along with empty food containers and plastic wrapping from food items, mostly cheap snacks and candy from the local IGA. The place looked and smelled like the inside of a dumpster.

The disorder made it difficult for him to negotiate a path to the separate bedroom, not much bigger than a walk-in closet. The first thing he noticed was a two-handled walker beside a twin bed. On the bed a middle-aged man wearing dirty blue jeans and a gray sweatshirt lay face down on the bed, a cast-iron monstrosity from a century ago.

He saw immediately what Antonio had meant when he said Jackson was indisposed. The sheets were brown with filth, as though they had never been washed. On the bedside table sat an empty bottle of vodka and a large tumbler half full of what he guessed was vodka: the colorless, odorless, tasteless liquid preferred by hard-core drunks.

Fernando grabbed the man's shoulder and shook him gently at first and then more roughly when he didn't get a response. "Clint?"

"Get offa me, motherfucker...." Clint moaned.

He tried again. "Wake up, this is the police. We need to ask you some questions."

"Lemme go, I'll kick your ass...." With that, Clint swung his arm back wildly at him, knocking over the empty bottle of vodka and the tumbler, which shattered on the floor beside the bed.

"Suit yourself," Fernando said. "We'll try this again down at the station—and it won't be voluntary."

Leaving the broken glass on the floor as a wake-up call for Jackson when he stepped out of bed, he returned to the living area. He found a stack of mail on the kitchen counter, its tiles cracked and broken revealing the plywood underneath. Some of the mail was opened and some of it still sealed. Mostly ads and bills of one kind or another, although he spotted a notice addressed to a Clint Jackson from Four Corners Enterprises, an oil and fracking company, concerning a disability claim Jackson had filed against them.

The notice informed Jackson that Four Corners Enterprises had denied his request for lack of medical reports supporting his claim. So apparently Jackson had been a working man once, not the hopeless drunk and derelict he appeared to be today. He had lots of questions he wanted to ask Sleeping Beauty, but for that he would have to wait for Jackson to sober up, which might take some time given his present condition.

He wrote down the name of the fracking company in his pocket notebook and then returned to the main house where only Antonio remained. Miguel and Teresa had finished their work and taken the body of Tom Flynn to the morgue for an autopsy.

Antonio frowned. "What a shithole this place is. Hard to imagine a cesspool like this on East Alameda."

Fernando nodded. "I want you to keep track of Jackson. As soon as he's sober, bring him in for questioning. Right away, before he gets loaded again."

"Will do."

"Right away, because your window of opportunity will be brief. I don't imagine Clint spends much of his day sober."

The big man laughed.

"And Antonio, check out Maria Lujan's son, Luis. He has an open wound on his forehead. Something about him bothers me. Maybe the way he reacted when he found out I was a cop."

2

Fernando sat in his office looking through the leather-bound journal they'd found on Tom Flynn's bed. Forensics had finished with the book, finding several sets of fingerprints, none of which matched known scumbags. So it was his to examine at the moment so long as he used latex gloves. The gloves made it more difficult to separate the yellowed pages.

He'd assumed correctly. Alton Flynn, Tom Flynn's grandfather, had written the journal while working with amateur archaeologist Richard Wetherill excavating Chaco Canyon. The journal began in 1896 and recorded their excavations at Pueblo Bonito, the largest ruin in Chaco Canyon. By contract Wetherill sent most of the artifacts they looted back east to their sponsors but managed to keep some to sell at a trading post they built along the rear wall of Bonito. A few years later their trading post was shut down by the government when Congress passed the Antiquities Act in 1906, making it illegal to alter or remove anything from national monuments, which Chaco Canyon officially became in 1907.

The last entry before the missing page, written on 23 August 1906, mentioned Wetherill's plan to hide a cache of the more valuable jewelry and pottery to sell at their trading post. The journal resumed with an entry on 6 September concerned with Wetherill's homestead and ranching activities in the canyon and never again mentioned the hidden cache. The journal ended on 22 June 1910, the day Wetherill was shot and killed by a Navajo man.

The entry read: "R.W. killed. Grudge. Chis-Chilling Begay."

He closed the journal and placed it carefully in the top drawer of his desk and then leaned back in his chair reflecting. If the murderer had killed Tom Flynn to get information about this hidden cache of artifacts, it would have to be someone who knew Flynn. That is, someone who knew of the journal's existence. Even so, the theory seemed crazy to him since the Antiquities Act made it a federal crime to dig in places like Chaco. After all, Chaco Canyon was a UNESCO World Heritage Site. What fool would be so brazen as to dig illegally in a World Heritage Site?

The phone interrupted his thoughts. "Fernando, it's Antonio. I'm bringing in Clint Jackson. I found him sober this morning. Mean as hell, but sober. I'll be there in a few minutes. Prepare yourself, he's a real piece of work."

"Okay, don't let him get near a bottle," Fernando said.

He prepared by looking through the notes in his pocket notebook. He wanted to refresh his memory by checking the name of the oil and fracking company Clint had worked for before his accident and subsequent disability.

He waited patiently, curious to see what a sober Clint Jackson looked like.

When they arrived, he heard the two men arguing all the way down the hall to his office. "Get your hands off me, you big sonofabitch," Jackson snapped at Antonio, who was physically herding him into the office.

"Just calm down," Antonio replied, giving him a final shove through the office door.

Jackson cursed and shoved his walker back out into the hallway, walking on his own over to a chair. He wore the same dirty jeans and gray sweatshirt he had worn yesterday. He smelled rancid, like bad booze and vomit, like he'd slept overnight in a port-o-let.

Fernando resisted the urge to hold his nose.

If this was Jackson's sober, it didn't look much different than Jackson's intoxicated. The old man's thinning brown hair was sticking up every which way, and his face was overgrown with patches of uneven stubble. Upright, he looked to be in his early fifties, but he could have been younger, given his sorry condition.

"Who are you?" Jackson asked.

Fernando introduced himself.

"So what the hell do you want? Why do you drag me all the way down here?" he spit out. "I got my rights. You can't just jerk me around whenever you feel like it!"

"Please. Be seated. I need to ask you some questions about Tom

Flynn's murder. We think he was murdered last Saturday night, four days ago. Were you with him that night?"

"Saturday? No. He'd been sick for about a week and wasn't drinking. I had to drink alone."

"What was wrong with him?" Fernando asked.

"How the hell am I supposed to know? He was losing weight and feeling sick, that's all he told me."

"So you were home alone Saturday night?"

"Yeah, sleeping."

"Drunk, you mean," Antonio snapped.

"Piss off! What's it to you?"

Fernando tried again. "Have you noticed anyone else around the house recently? Any strangers you hadn't seen before?"

"No! I told you, he'd been sick all week!"

Antonio was getting angry now, which didn't bode well for Jackson. "Watch your mouth, old timer!"

"Fuck you! I'll kick your ass!" Clint sputtered, turning to face Antonio. "I've licked bigger men than you!"

"That's enough!" Fernando shouted, bolting up in his seat and looking Jackson squarely in the eye.

"Look, we can do this the easy way, here in the office, or I can have you held for questioning overnight. That means no booze. Have you ever seen a man go through DTs? It's not a pretty sight. Makes you feel like your skin is on fire, like your head is about to explode. Some people try to jump through windows, others bang their heads against a wall. You go crazy with pain. Is that how you want to spend the next twenty-four hours? Because if it is, I'll have Antonio escort you to booking right now and you can find out for yourself what it's like to go through DTs in a jail cell not much bigger than a closet!"

Jackson said nothing.

Fernando sat down again and continued. "First, I want to know about your relationship with Tom Flynn. Were you renting his guest house?"

"No...we were friends, good buddies. He let me stay there rent-free. We liked to drink together."

"So I saw," Fernando said. "By the way, what happened to your legs?"

"It's my back. I fell and smashed three vertebrae on the job. I worked on an oil rig up in San Juan County. Fuckers won't even pay me disability." He reached around and touched his lower back. "The doctors want to fuse the vertebrae and inject cement. I won't have it. Bunch of fucking quacks."

"The oil company, would that be Four Corners Enterprises?"

"That's them, the cheap motherfuckers."

Fernando nodded. "Okay. Now tell me again, where were you the night Flynn was murdered?"

"Like I said, I was sleeping."

"Do you know why anyone would want to kill Flynn? Want him dead?"

"I suppose it was because he was from an old Santa Fe family. They thought he had money. His father was on City Council and his grandfather worked with Richard Wetherill, for fuck's sake."

"But he was broke, a pauper. He was reduced to selling wooden trinkets on the Plaza."

"Yeah, but whoever killed him didn't know that. I'm telling you, he was from an old Santa Fe family. That means something around here. You should know that, you look like a damned Mexican!"

Fernando frowned. He was used to lowlifes like Clint calling him a Mexican, but he resented the hell out of it. His family had been in Santa Fe for over three hundred years. Trash like Clint knew nothing about Santa Fe.

Still, he held his tongue.

"What do you know about the leather-bound journal we found laying on Flynn's bed?"

Jackson's eyes opened wide. "What about the journal?"

"We found it open on his bed with a page torn out. Whoever ransacked the room and killed Flynn may have wanted that page. Do you have any idea what's on the page? Had Flynn mentioned the journal recently?"

Jackson shook his head. "That's what I'm trying to tell you, he was from an old Santa Fe family. I told him to throw that goddamn journal away before it caused him problems. He was always bragging about it and trying to sell it to raise money. Hah! Who would pay good money for crap like that?"

"What about the missing page? What was on that page?"

"How would I know? I never read the damned thing. What's wrong with you, you're not listening to what I'm telling you. Why do you continue asking me all these goddamn questions?"

Jackson's hands had started twitching in his lap. He needed a drink real bad, or else he would be climbing the walls and going into DTs before long.

"Listen, do you happen to have a bottle here? Can you give me a little something to hold me over?"

"No...but I'll make a deal with you," Fernando said. "I'll let you go for now if you'll agree to contact me if you think of anything else, or if you notice any strangers hanging around your house."

"What do you mean?"

"Well, someone killed Ton Flynn. You could be in danger too. If he didn't find what he was looking for, the murderer may be back."

Jackson looked around nervously, from Fernando to Antonio. "Yeah, sure, whatever you say," he said, getting up slowly and steadying himself by holding on to the chair. Then he turned and walked into the hallway, grabbing his walker and waiting for Antonio to drive him back home.

Antonio came over to his desk before leaving. "We checked out the Luis Lujan kid like you wanted. He's clean, no record to speak of. We found only one incident last Thursday. His girlfriend called in a domestic violence complaint against him. He says the argument got physical and that's when he got the wound on his forehead. The girlfriend wouldn't press charges, so the complaint was dismissed. I thought you should know."

"Thanks. Can you drive him home? I think Clint's about to come unglued unless he gets a drink soon."

"Not a problem. Glad to get rid of him."

3

Fernando and Estelle had been working together in their garden after dinner, one of their ways of relaxing before bedtime. They had clipped the stalks of their hollyhocks and weeded their precious rose bushes. When they finished, Estelle had gone inside their adobe home to freshen up and then get ready for bed. He stayed behind, wanting to sit for a few minutes on the patio, watching the moon rise east of the city, over the giant cottonwoods that lined the acequia behind their property.

Their patio was his quiet place, his refuge from a troubled world, from all the problems he encountered every day at his job. Six months earlier he would have stayed on the patio to smoke a comforting cigarette or two, but no more. He was a new man, a healthier man since he'd stopped smoking.

The beeping of his cellphone interrupted his reveries. Who would be calling at this late hour, half past nine on a weekday?

"Mr. Fernando?" came a vaguely familiar voice. "This is Maria Lujan. I want to tell you that someone is in Mr. Tom's house right now. I just took some food to Mr. Clint and I saw a man with a flashlight walking through the house. I don't know who he is or what to think...."

"Was it Clint Jackson?"

"No, I talk to Mr. Clint in the small house. He says to mind my own business and get out, so I be safe. I'm afraid to ask any more questions or go into Mr. Tom's house."

"Okay, thanks, I'll check it out."

He decided not to tell Estelle since he would be back before she missed him. No sense upsetting her at this late hour. Instead, he hurried around to the driveway and climbed into his Plymouth.

It took only minutes to drive the few blocks to East Alameda and cross the bridge. He saw a couple of cars parked farther up the street but none near the Flynn property. He cut the engine and drifted into the driveway. He closed the car door quietly and walked slowly, cautiously toward the front of the house, not knowing what to expect. No sign of anyone inside, so he continued around to the side of the house. There he thought he heard something, like someone rummaging through a closet. Freezing, he listened carefully, but the sound seemed to have stopped.

He inched closer to the side window of the bedroom. Through the drawn shade he saw a splash of light, a faint beam from a flashlight inside moving through the room like a ghost. So Maria Lujan had been right, Mr. Tom had a nighttime visitor looking for something.

But what? Something he'd missed earlier?

He crept around behind the house, remembering Maria Lujan saying that Flynn kept his rear door unlocked. From the walkway he noticed the guesthouse was dark and closed up tight, as though Clint Jackson had gone out or was otherwise indisposed. Since Maria Lujan had seen him there twenty or thirty minutes earlier, he suspected Jackson was drunk by now, passed out in his bed.

A nearly full moon bathed the back yard in a pale ghostly light as he moved slowly toward the patio. The leaves of the cottonwoods on Canyon Road glistened in the moonlight. No wind, no sound, only dead silence. He could have been walking through a graveyard, it was that quiet. He began to feel a bit uneasy. He didn't consider himself superstitious, but then again, he wasn't all that comfortable with prowling around a dead man's house in the dark.

In this city of ghosts, built as it was over the bones of the inhabitants of Ogapoge Pueblo who settled here over a thousand years ago, you never knew who—or what—you were going to encounter after the sun set.

He tried to shake off the uneasy feeling. He wished he'd taken the time to put on his uniform and his holster. He'd left without arming himself against whatever awaited him in the darkness of the Flynn house. But it was too late now. There was no going back.

He edged closer to the door, listening for any movement inside. He heard nothing.

He tried the door, opening it just a crack and looking into the darkness. Again, nothing. So he gently opened the door just enough for him to squeeze through. Now the light from the moon splashed on the wooden floor of the house. He worried the light would alert the intruder, but he could do nothing about moonlight. So he stepped inside quickly and closed the door behind him. Then he crept forward again, stopping after every step to listen for movement.

Proceeding like this, one step at a time, he kept one hand on the kitchen wall to find his way to the opening of the bedroom. He figured the intruder would be in the bedroom, if he or she were still here. The bedroom was where the box of papers had been tossed on the floor and where anything of value would be stored.

Then he heard a floorboard squeak in the direction of the bedroom. He stopped to listen. Maybe he'd imagined the sound, maybe not. He waited for a few seconds and then took another small step. Now he could feel the door jamb along the wall. He was getting close. The room seemed darker than the kitchen, with all curtains and shades drawn. He could see nothing, not even rough shapes in the darkness. He closed his eyes tightly, hoping they would better adjust to the darkness. When that didn't work, he threw caution to the wind and took a step forward into the blackness.

Suddenly he felt movement off to his left. It was just a slight change in air current, nothing more. He was turning toward the movement when the blow came, like a burst of lightning, smashing into the side of his skull and pitching him sideways onto the floor of the bedroom.

Everything went black.

Much later, as he began to regain consciousness, he felt his nose rubbing against the rough floorboards and wetness under his chin. He tried to move, but his body did not respond to the message. He tried again. Finally he managed to roll over on his back, looking up into the shooting sparks and the static that rippled the darkness before his eyes. The back of his head pounded, and his chin felt raw where he had scraped it on the floor.

Remembering where he was, he began to panic. He had to get up before his assailant attacked him again. He struggled to his knees, and then bracing himself against the wall tried to stand up. When his knees buckled, he sat back down on his ass and leaned back against the wall. He chided himself for not being prepared. He should have brought his weapon.

Not a pretty picture for a police detective.

Just how long he sat there before recouping his strength he had no way of knowing. On his second try to stand up he managed to get to his feet and take stock of his wounds. His face was scratched and hurt like hell. Worse, though, the side of his head was bleeding—he knew because when he touched it his hand came back wet with blood. That was the bad news. The good news was that his assailant had left the kitchen door wide open when he fled, providing enough moonlight for him to see his way to the door.

The fresh night air invigorated him somewhat. Still unsteady on his feet, he made his way around the house to the driveway, where he found another unwelcome sight. Someone, presumably his assailant, had taken a key or some metal object and scratched into the side of his Plymouth a parting message that served as one last blow to his self-esteem: DEAD MAN.

Now that pissed him off. Big time. How was he supposed to drive around Santa Fe with DEAD MAN scratched on the side of his car? A police detective.

No, he would need to have the car repainted, which would probably cost more than a 2007 Plymouth Acclaim was worth.

More important at the moment was to get home quickly before Estelle woke up and discovered his absence. If she discovered he had gone out this late at night, not to mention been attacked by a possible murderer, she would start up again about how he should retire from the department immediately while he still had his health, by which she meant while he was still breathing! That argument was not something he wanted to repeat anytime soon.

So filled with remorse on all accounts he climbed into DEAD MAN and drove back home, parking at the end of the driveway so as not to make any noise. As stealthily as possible he entered the back door and tiptoed to the hall bathroom on the opposite side of the house from the master bedroom.

Then he undressed and showered, rinsing the blood out of his short gray hair and washing the wound with antiseptic soap. He didn't think the wound was bad enough to require a trip to the emergency room for stitches. He knew from past experience that scalp wounds bled like a sonofabitch even if they were only surface. If he kept it clean, the wound would heal.

His nose and chin were scratched from his fall, so he stood under the shower and let the water rinse over his face and left it at that, no antiseptic soap or ointments. The scratches would heal in good time. At his age he didn't give a damn about how he looked, which is why he always avoided looking in the mirror at his brown, wrinkled face.

He hid his blood stained clothing in the bottom of Estelle's laundry basket, thinking he could come up with some story explaining the blood if and when she noticed it. He'd used the bloody nose explanation with success before, so he might be able to use something similar. And this time he had scratches and bruises for supporting evidence. Walked into a door? Tripped in the garden? He'd think of something when the time came.

Reassured by his plan, he crept down the hallway into their bedroom and lay down beside Estelle. Safe and sound. He hoped.

4

Fernando pulled into the parking lot beside the Washington Avenue station late the next morning, finding Antonio and Manny Alvarez already on their way out. They stopped when they saw him park, staring at the DEAD MAN slogan scratched on the side of his Plymouth, amused by the sight. "I see you've detailed your car," Manny said as Fernando climbed out of the Plymouth.

Manny stood a foot shorter and weighed a hundred pounds less than Antonio. He was a real wise ass, always joking at someone else's expense. Still, Fernando had warmed up to Manny. If nothing else, you could always count on Manny for a little humor, which was much appreciated in their line of work.

Fernando laughed in spite of himself. "I knew you'd like it, Manny."

"Jesus, what happened to your face?" Antonio asked.

"A little accident, I'm okay."

They peppered him with so many questions that against his better judgment he finally told them what had happened at Flynn's house during the night, beginning with the phone call from Maria Lujan and ending up on the floor with a nasty headache and a scratched face.

Manny got serious for a moment. "You should have called for backup."

"Did you get a look at the guy?" Antonio asked. "Was it Clint Jackson, that miserable old fucker?"

"I don't know. I couldn't see anything, it was too dark. But I don't think it was Clint, because Maria Lujan said she talked to him in the guesthouse after she saw the light in Flynn's house. That was just a few minutes before I got there."

Manny ran his hand over the DEAD MAN scratch. "Man, you got

a score to settle with the punk who did this, even if the car is a piece of shit. I'll tell you what, my cousin Jorge owns a shop on Cerrillos Road and he could fix you up in no time. He would repaint DEAD MAN for a couple hundred dollars, I'm sure. Be good as new. You just say the word, bro."

"I'll let you know," Fernando said.

With that, he left his two best friends in the department and walked into the station. Linda was on the phone, but she raised her hand in greeting when he walked by to his office. He wanted some privacy this morning, so he closed the door behind him. So far the only lead he had in the Flynn murder investigation was the missing page of Alton Flynn's journal. If the page was what the murderer wanted, then it must have included details on the whereabouts of Wetherill's hidden artifacts. Why else would the thief want it bad enough to murder Flynn?

Unless, of course, Flynn had been murdered for an entirely different reason. Maybe it was simply a burglary gone wrong. Maybe Flynn had surprised an intruder looking for money or goods to resell. Who knew?

He could speculate all the wanted, but it didn't change the fact that the missing page of the journal was the only lead he had. To pursue that angle, he needed more information about Wetherill and his trading post at Pueblo Bonito. He Googled Wetherill and found the Wetherill Family Archive with lots of useful information and photos of Richard Wetherill's life in Chaco Canyon. He found an 1896 photo of Wetherill's earliest trading post, built against the rear wall of Pueblo Bonito. According to the explanatory material accompanying the photo, Wetherill and his crew dug through the rear wall of the ruin, thereby accessing several rooms of Bonito to use as part of his trading post.

He took the Flynn journal out of his desk drawer and reread the daily entries leading up to the missing page. The entries seemed to imply that Wetherill intended to hide his cache of artifacts in or around his trading post. That could mean the artifacts were buried either inside Bonito or outside on the perimeter. With the photograph it should be possible to determine the exact location of the structure in what remained of the ruin.

He printed a copy of the photo and put it in his back pocket. Right now, he wanted to run over to the Great Burrito Company for a cup of coffee and then return to Flynn's house, to see if last night's assailant had left behind any clues to his identity. Manny was right, he had a score to settle with the punk who had defaced his Plymouth. DEAD MAN indeed!

His plan for the morning lasted all of thirty seconds. Linda stopped him at the door, having just finished her phone call. "Fernando, wait! The Chief has another assignment for you. He just left for the City Council meeting. Do you remember Pete Chavez... used to work for us back in the twenty tens?"

"Yeah, vaguely. He quit to do something else."

Linda nodded. "He's been working as a park ranger at Chaco Canyon for the past few years. His body was found yesterday morning with his head bashed in by a shovel. We got the call about an hour ago from the ranger in charge, a guy by the name of Jim Murphy. He said Pete was making the nightly security rounds and didn't return to staff barracks. The other rangers sent out a search team early yesterday and found him dead in one of the ruins. Murphy thinks Pete surprised some looters digging illegally in the park and the looters killed him."

"Sorry to hear that. How do they know he was killed with a shovel?"

"They found a bloody shovel next to the body. In the ruin."

Fernando nodded. "Which ruin?"

"Pueblo Bonito."

That got his attention. "No kidding? I'll be damned."

He found it too much of a coincidence to be a coincidence. Maybe he'd been wrong to downplay the journal and its missing page. Suddenly the possibility that someone searching for Wetherill's hidden artifacts murdered Flynn didn't seem so farfetched.

Linda raised her hand, indicating she had more information. "So here's the scoop. The FBI has jurisdiction over illegal digging at a national park, which is a violation of the Antiquities Act and a federal crime. It turns out the FBI office in Albuquerque wants to send a field agent to Chaco this morning. The Chief wants you to go along to help with the murder investigation. Got it? They want you to pick up the agent at noon today in Albuquerque. She'll be waiting at the Albuquerque office."

"She?" he asked.

"Yeah, you got a problem with that?" Linda challenged him.

He shrugged, knowing he'd best hold his tongue. Linda didn't go off very often, but when she did, watch out. Anyway, he hadn't worked with many FBI agents who were women, so he didn't know if he did or did not have a problem.

"Here's the address. It's on the Eastern side of Albuquerque, off

Tramway," Linda said, and handed him a slip of paper. The office was on Luecking Park Avenue N.E., which meant absolutely nothing to him.

"Can you hook me up with a cruiser?"

"Already done," Linda said, handing him a set of keys. Then she looked him in the eye. "And Fernando, be nice, okay. The last thing we need is for the FBI to think the Santa Fe Police Department is full of sexist pigs, even if we are, okay?"

He gave her a mock salute and headed for the Great Burrito Company. At least he had time for a cup of coffee and a trip home to tell Estelle he had to drive to Chaco Canyon on business.

Estelle would not be happy.

He checked out the unmarked cruiser Linda had reserved for him from their vehicle lot and drove directly home. After placating Estelle as best he could, promising to be safe and to call every evening, he packed a shaving kit and overnight bag just in case they were delayed and had to spend the night somewhere. Wouldn't it be fun explaining that to Estelle? Especially if she found out he was traveling with an FBI agent that happened to be a woman.

Estelle had kept a close eye on him ever since his brief affair with Linda back in the day. Estelle had forgiven him once but made it crystal clear she would not do it twice.

The drive to Albuquerque on I-25 was as boring as ever, primarily because he'd done it so many times. After La Bajada Hill the land flattened out until you approached the Santo Domingo and San Felipe pueblos. There the reddish, triangular shaped hills dotted with juniper and piñon trees broke up the monotony and provided a bit of respite before entering the ugly outskirts of Albuquerque, a maze of strip malls and car lots. It took him a good forty minutes to find Luecking Park Avenue. By the time he arrived at the Albuquerque FBI office it was well past noon. He was late, not a good way to start off.

The nondescript office building looked nothing like what he expected a law enforcement building to look like. More like a typical office building that housed small businesses. Much to his surprise he found the agent assigned to accompany him sitting in a small waiting area just inside the front door, a tall striking woman holding what looked like an overnight bag in her lap. Her eyes zeroed in on him as he walked through the door and into the corridor. She was obviously

Navajo, with raven black hair braided to the middle of her back. The fact that she, too, had brought an overnight bag was not a good sign.

"You're late," she said, and introduced herself as Patricia Begay. She looked to be in her late thirties.

"Fernando Lopez." He extended his hand, which she promptly ignored.

She hoisted up her bag and walked swiftly outside. He followed, with not a word exchanged.

When they were seated in the cruiser, she took a New Mexico state map out of her bag and opened it on her lap. "Take I-Twenty-five north to Five-Fifty."

He drove out of the parking lot and headed for I-25.

A few minutes later when they turned onto 550 west, she said, "Take Five-Fifty northwest to County Road Seventy-nine hundred near Nageezi. Then turn right on County Road Seventy-Nine-Fifty to Chaco Canyon. It should take about two hours and fifteen minutes."

He studied her out of the corner of his eye, trying to get a read on her. Usually he was a pretty good judge of character, but Patricia Begay eluded him. She seemed fixated on detail and eager to avoid eye contact with him. Was she autistic?

Outside of Bernalillo, when the cityscape changed to red mesas with the peaks of the Jemez mountain range pink and white in the distance, she seemed to close her eyes as though meditating. He grew more and more uncomfortable as they drove on in silence. Finally out of frustration he asked, "So what do you know about the digging at Chaco Canyon?"

Her eyes opened. "It's illegal."

He laughed. "Yeah, I know, but do you have any more information? Did the digging damage the ruin? Was anything taken?"

"Not to my knowledge."

He was confused. "Are you angry about something?"

"I'm not happy about driving to Chaco, if that's what you mean."

"I feel the same way."

"I doubt it," she said. "I'm supposed to be the Bureau liaison to the Tribal Police on all the Indian reservations. The other agents--all of whom are men, of course--refuse to have anything to do with the Tribal Police. It's an impossible job, given the number of reservations in the state of New Mexico, not to mention all the ruins and archaeological sites connected to the tribes."

"Why'd you take the job?" Fernando asked.

"Good question. At the time I was working for the Tribal Police in Crownpoint and thought the FBI would be a promotion. I took the job at Crownpoint right after graduating from the Navajo Nation Police Academy in Chinle. I should have stayed put--I was happy there. If I had, I wouldn't be on my way to a place I've always tried to avoid."

"Why's that?"

She did not respond.

He didn't know what to say, so he kept his mouth shut for several miles. He decided not to tell her about his experience as a young Chicano cop on a police force run by Anglos. Not all that different from hers.

Finally he said, "I was given the assignment because Pete Chavez formerly worked for the Santa Fe Police Department. And whoever killed him may be involved in another murder investigation I'm working on in Santa Fe."

She nodded but said nothing.

They stopped at the McDonalds in Cuba for a late lunch because it was fast and conveniently located on the highway. They exchanged only small talk while they ate their salads with spicy chicken, the only item on the menu that looked remotely appetizing. He loaded up on coffee, needing caffeine for the long drive ahead, whereas Patricia seemed oblivious to the food and the drink, not to mention the conversation. Finally he gave up the effort to make small talk. She clearly had a lot on her mind, more than just the trip to Chaco Canyon.

When they finished their meal, they climbed back in the cruiser and continued north on Highway 550. They skirted the foothills of the Jemez Mountains and climbed onto the flat Colorado Plateau. Approaching Nageezi they passed rows of oil and fracking companies along the highway, their rigs breaking up the harsh beauty of the natural landscape.

He almost missed the turnoff to Chaco looking at the ugly oil rigs. He saw the sign at the last second and swerved to the left, turning onto County Road 7900. Patricia stared at him.

"Sorry."

He drove quickly over the paved leg of the road to Chaco. That changed when he turned right onto County Road 7950, the unmaintained gravel road leading into Chaco Canyon. He had to slow down to a crawl over the rough road to avoid deep ruts and animals, goats and cows, grazing along the road. The sage and saltbush along the winding road glistened silver in the late afternoon light.

He kept his eyes on the road, steering from side to side to avoid the deeper ruts. Sometimes he had to come to a complete stop and then ease over a particularly deep rut or an elevated ridge of rock. The road seemed to go on forever.

When they finally drove though the stone gates of the Chaco Culture Historical Park onto a paved road, Patricia mumbled something that he didn't catch. She turned to him.

"Pull over here, please."

He stopped the car on the side of the road as she requested.

She climbed out of the cruiser without offering an explanation.

He watched her cross the road to a trailhead off to the left and then stop. She appeared to speak, saying a few words to someone or something. Then she slowly raised her hands into the sky. When she finished, she paused for a few moments and then returned to the car, again without explanation.

She noticed him staring at her. "I said a Navajo prayer, a prayer asking for our protection," she said finally. "We'll need it."

He waited but she offered no explanation.

Okay, he said to himself and then drove off again. Just past a campground the road curved around to staff headquarters, built back in a box canyon on the right side of the road. They had been told to report to Unit #5, Jim Murphy's unit. The staff barracks looked like a 1960s-era motel with a porch light and a sitting chair outside of every door, all lined up in a neat row. He parked the cruiser in the parking lot, and the two of them grabbed their overnight bags and headed for #5.

Halfway to the unit, the door opened and out walked a tall thin man waving to them. "Come on in," the tall man said, coming out to greet them. "Man, are we glad to see you. Didn't know it would take you so long to get here, but no problem. Betty and I waited for you."

They saw an older woman in the open doorway now, waiting for them inside unit #5.

Jim Murphy shook their hands. "Fernando, you can stay with me. And Patricia, we have you with Betty Madsen over there. She's the only woman currently on staff at Chaco. We can accommodate you for as long as you need to be here, providing you're willing to rough it a bit. We're only one level above camping," he said, laughing. "If that."

"Thanks," Fernando said, looking at Patricia. That they might need long-term accommodations was news to him. Bad news.

"Won't be a problem for me," she said. "I grew up in a hogan without electricity or running water."

"Good, you'll feel right at home. Come on in and we can talk. I'll bring you up to speed."

They followed Jim into his unit, a two-room efficiency with a separate bedroom. He and Patricia sat together on a beat-up sofa, while Betty took the only chair in the living area. Jim remained standing, too revved up to bother with bringing in a stool from the kitchen counter.

"I'm really glad you're here," Jim said, speaking rapidly. "We need to come up with a plan of action. We've dealt with looters before but never with murderers. I'm worried about the safety of my crew, not to mention their morale. You can imagine. All this has been very upsetting to all of us."

Jim shook his head. "I still can't believe what happened to Pete. His face was beaten to a pulp and his head was twisted nearly off his shoulders. I'm sure his neck was broken. I can still see him lying in the dirt. Why would someone do that to another person? I mean, Pete was just doing his job as a park ranger. I don't know what to do now. Do we need to carry weapons when we do our morning and evening security checks in order to protect ourselves? Has it come to that?"

"Good question," Fernando said.

"I didn't sign on for that. None of us did."

Fernando nodded. "Do you have any weapons here?"

"We have one rifle, which we keep locked in a gun safe. We've only used it once since I've been here. To put down a rabid elk terrorizing the campground."

"Tell us how you discovered Pete's body and what you found," Patricia said, cutting to the chase. "You said the looters who did this were digging in the ruin, correct?"

"Yes, that's right. They were digging in one of the small rooms inside the rear wall. They left a small pit, about three feet deep. They also busted through the rear wall with a pick-axe or sledge hammer, something heavy."

"Did they find anything? Could you tell?"

Jim began to pace back and forth in the small unit while he talked. "I don't think so. Usually you see broken pottery shards and fragments when something has been uncovered. Not here. The site was clean."

"That means they'll be back," Patricia said.

Jim stopped pacing. He didn't like what he was hearing.

"So tell us again how you found Pete. What you saw when you approached Pueblo Bonito."

Now Jim grabbed a stool from the kitchen counter and carried it into the living area and sat down. As he began to repeat his account of discovering Pete's body, his cellphone rang.

He took the phone out of his pants pocket. "This is Jim Murphy."

Listening, he stood up and began pacing again. "Where? What was he doing? Okay, we'll be right up!"

Jim turned to them. "That was Ernie from maintenance. They found someone hiding behind the garage on the mesa. The guy has a shovel in the back of his car. Let's go!"

Part Two: Chaco Canyon

5

They rushed outside and climbed into an open staff jeep covered with white dust. Jim drove, while Patricia rode shotgun and Fernando sat in back. Betty stayed behind to help out at the visitor center. Jim gunned the engine and drove out of the parking lot, turning left onto the road out of Chaco. He shot past the stone gate and up a long hill to the top of the mesa, where he turned left onto a service road that took them around behind the visitor center and staff barracks to a maintenance area.

As they drove into the area he saw the park's water tank and electric grid as well as a large Quonset hut. The open doors of the corrugated steel building revealed road maintenance vehicles and park supplies and construction materials. Ernie stood outside the Quonset hut waiting for them.

Jim slammed on his brakes and jumped out of the jeep. "Where is he?"

"Carl's got him cornered around back."

Ernie motioned for them to follow him. He took them behind the Quonset hut where two pickups blocked a gray Subaru Outback. Carl, Ernie's co-worker, stood off to the side with his arms folded across his chest staring at the young man inside the Outback. Jim and Ernie joined Carl.

Fernando and Patricia took their time, studying the lay of the land.

Walking up to the rear of the Outback Fernando saw a shovel and an empty wooden crate in its back storage area. The shovel looked brand new, as if it had never been used. He didn't get a clear view of the young man until he circled around to the driver's window and looked in at none other than Luis Lujan, Maria Lujan's son. He took a step back, not believing his eyes. "What the hell are you doing here?"

Luis looked up at him, a darkly handsome young man with close-cropped hair who looked to be in his twenties. Wearing a T-shirt and shorts, he was dressed for relaxation, not for digging in a dusty ruin.

"Answer me, what are you doing here?" Fernando shouted.

"I took the wrong turn. I'm looking for the canyon. You know, for a little hiking." Luis forced a laugh.

He didn't buy it. "So why are you up here hiding behind the maintenance building?"

"I was studying my map." Luis held up a map of the canyon.

Patricia walked up to the open window and looked in at Luis. She moved directly to the issue at hand. "Why do you have a shovel in the back of your vehicle? Have you been digging in the canyon?"

"No!" the kid shot back. The shovel's just in case I get stuck."

She shook her head. "That's an all-wheel drive vehicle, sir."

Luis seemed to shrink down in the seat. He looked tired, deflated, not the cocky young man Fernando had seen yelling at his mother back in Santa Fe.

"Sir, do you understand that digging in a national park is illegal? It's a violation of the Antiquities Act and carries a stiff penalty."

"I understand."

"What exactly were you looking for?" Patricia asked.

"I told you, I wasn't digging! I keep the shovel in back just in case I get stuck."

Patricia frowned. "Do you get stuck often? In an all-wheel drive vehicle?"

Luis did not respond.

Patricia stepped back from the car and motioned for everyone to join her off to the side. Fernando followed Ernie, Carl, and Jim. They gathered behind one of the pickups. "What do you all think?" she asked.

"I think he's lying," Ernie said. "We found him here about noon, but who knows how long he's been hiding there?"

Jim agreed. "Not only that, but it's hard to imagine anyone mistaking this for the entrance to the park. You can actually SEE the park straight ahead when you turn off on the service road to come up here. He's lying."

"Okay, but there's no evidence of him actually digging in the park, so what do we do with him?" She looked at him. "Fernando?"

When he didn't respond, she made the decision herself. "Let's kick him out with a warning. Tell him this area is off-limits to the public and if we see him here again we'll arrest him for trespassing."

The others agreed.

Fernando listened while she confronted Luis, telling him to stay away from the maintenance area or he would be arrested for trespassing and taken to the San Juan County Jail.

Luis agreed, seemingly contrite, and drove off as soon as Carl and Ernie moved their pickups. They all watched the gray Outback weave its way down the service road to County Road 7950 and turn left, back toward Albuquerque and Santa Fe.

Fernando was troubled by the reappearance of Luis and by the possible connection between the murders of Tom Flynn and Pete Chavez. He didn't believe in coincidence. Not when it came to murder.

"I wouldn't be surprised if we saw Luis again," he said, following Patricia and Jim Murphy to the jeep.

"What do you mean?"

"Just this, I ran into him yesterday at the house in Santa Fe where we found the body of Tom Flynn. Flynn was murdered, apparently by someone looking for a journal written by Flynn's grandfather Alton, who worked with Richard Wetherill excavating Chaco Canyon. The journal contained information about a cache of artifacts Wetherill hid in Pueblo Bonito near where he had his trading post."

Patricia looked confused. "What was Luis doing there?"

"He'd come to pick up his mother, who worked for Flynn."

Jim raised his hand. "I don't understand. What are you suggesting? That Luis and whoever he's working with are trying to find artifacts supposedly hidden by Wetherill?"

It's a possibility," Fernando said. "That would explain his appearance here. And it would explain the recent digging in Bonito."

"What kind of artifacts? Do you have anything more specific?"

"No, because the critical page was ripped out of the journal."

Jim nodded. "Well, at any rate, if Luis is working with whoever killed Pete, we're going to need your help. We'll need your protection on our evening security check especially. That can be scary as hell in the dark anyway. Not so much on the morning check. By then the looters would be gone. So can you guys stay a few days?"

They looked at each other.

Fernando shrugged. "Well, I need to get back to Santa Fe, but I suppose I could stay a day or so. What about you?"

"I can stay, no problem," Patricia said.

"Good! Then it's settled!" Jim jumped into the jeep and waited for them to do the same.

Jim waved goodbye to Ernie and Carl, turned sharply and shot off in a cloud of dust. When they pulled up to the staff barracks, he led them into his unit and offered them cold drinks.

"I can organize an impromptu get-together tomorrow after we close so I can introduce you to everyone. There's not enough time tonight. Let's eat a light dinner and then do the evening security check. I'll show you what we do every night when we close the park."

Jim made sandwiches and served them with cold beer. After dinner he handed each of them a map of the canyon and described the major ruins in the canyon and on the mesas. When they had their bearings, they waited for sunset and whatever the night might bring.

6

A nearly full moon hung over the canyon, splashing the ruins and cliffs in a pale yellow light as he and Patricia climbed into the staff jeep to accompany Jim on the nightly security check. Across the canyon floor the enormous mass of Fajada Butte towered above Chaco Wash like an enormous beast stalking the canyon. Shadows deepened into the interiors of the ruins, creating an air of mystery and danger for all who would enter the darkness. From Chacra Mesa to the east came the distant howl of coyotes hunting for rabbit and other small game.

They stopped at the park entrance just long enough for Jim to close and lock the gate behind them, and then they were off, driving slowly along the dark road into the deepening shadows. When the moon disappeared behind a cloud the entire canyon was plunged into thick darkness. When it appeared again they could see the moonlight reflecting off the ruins.

From the road it would be easy to spot any artificial lights among the ruins and thus any digging since looters would be unable to dig without adequate light, he reasoned. Jim drove slowly, deliberately so their collective eyes could sweep the entire length and breadth of the canyon.

They drove by Hungo Pavi and were approaching Chetro Ketl when Patricia suddenly pointed across the canyon toward South Mesa. "Look. See the lights over by Casa Rinconada?"

"Where?" Jim asked, slowing down.

"Looks like they're inside Rinconada," she said.

"Yes...I see it now!" Jim said, excitement in his voice.

Casa Rinconada was the largest Great Kiva in Chaco, with a 63-foot diameter and anterooms with underground tunnels leading into the kiva on both its north and south sides. Fernando knew the circular Great Kivas were used for public ceremonies, religious and otherwise. He also knew that whatever was happening there tonight wasn't meant to be a religious ceremony.

He saw what looked like a campfire flickering in the darkness.

Instantly Jim cut the engine and the lights on the jeep. They coasted to a stop on the road as another cloud overhead plunged the canyon into darkness. They waited until the cloud passed, and then Jim took his binoculars out of the glove compartment and studied the feeble, flickering light.

"Yes, the lights are definitely inside Rinconada."

Jim turned to face them. "Okay, here's the plan. We drive around the loop to Rinconada without lights. We park in the parking lot below the kiva and very quietly walk up the trail to the ruin. We want to keep the element of surprise, so it's important not to make any noise. You're both armed, so the two of you can take over at the top. Whatever occurs, it's your call. But be careful! Remember what happened to Pete Chavez. Okay?"

"And stick together," he added. "Let's don't get lost in the dark."

They drove in silence and without lights past Pueblo Bonito and over the bridge across Chaco Wash to the south side of the canyon. Jim slowed down to a crawl as they approached Casa Rinconada, the road in front of them resembling a pale silver ribbon stretching out into the darkness. Jim cut the engine altogether as they pulled into the parking lot and coasted to a stop. Opening and closing the doors of the jeep as quietly as possible, they began creeping up the trail, which meandered and then curved up a small knoll.

Fernando thought he heard a low moaning sound coming from the ruin, or maybe it was just the wind, he couldn't tell. Ahead of them they saw a pale swath of light and a thin plume of smoke dancing above the round, roofless kiva. Jim led the way, while he fell back, growing more anxious with every step. Patricia brought up the rear, hesitant. He understood why. Without any cover, they were sitting ducks on the trail in the moonlight.

Jim stopped when he reached the top and motioned for them to spread out around the monster kiva. Fernando moved to his right, toward the south entrance with its row of anterooms. Patricia remained on the trail, holding back.

Peering over the rim into the kiva, Fernando didn't know what he expected to see: ghosts, or just looters. Instead, he saw no one, only a fire burning in the ancient stone fire pit that was a thousand years old. Then he noticed the mirrors. Someone had placed mirrors at both the north and south underground entrances to the kiva, creating an eerie hall of mirrors effect, with the mirrors reflecting the fire and each other's reflection of the fire. The surreal effect mystified him. Why?

"There!" Patricia shouted, jolting him out of his thoughts. She pointed toward South Mesa, which towered above the kiva.

A flickering light was moving slowly toward the head of the South Mesa Trail, a flashlight or torch of some kind. It was too dark to see whoever or whatever was carrying the light. With a little luck they might be able to catch up with them.

"Well, shit!" Jim said. I can't do anything until I put out that fire." He ran back down the trail and brought back a canvas tarp that he rolled up and tossed into the kiva. Then he climbed down into the underground entryway and squeezed through the tiny, T-shaped door into the kiva. Grabbing the tarp, he threw it over the open pit and tried to smother the fire, which kept smoking under the tarp. Cursing, he pulled off the tarp and began scraping up handfuls of dirt and sand and tossing them on the coals. That helped, but not enough.

"Okay, turn your backs, ladies and gentlemen," Jim said, unzipping his pants and pissing on the coals. The smoke all but stopped now.

They laughed.

Jim threw more dirt on the fire and then dusted off his hands. Then he gathered up the two mirrors, cheap 20 by 24 inch mirrors that you could find at any home or hardware store, and squeezed back through the entryway and rejoined them on the trail. "Clever," he said, holding the mirrors up for them to admire. "Never seen that before."

Fernando noticed the light and its bearer had begun the long climb up South Mesa.

"Here," Jim said, handing him and Patricia each a small flashlight. "Follow me up the trail."

Jim led the way, jogging down the trail that ran west along the base of the cliff and then cut back sharply to the east and began climbing the imposing mesa. Even with a flashlight Fernando had trouble seeing the trail and avoiding the loose rocks that caused him to occasionally stumble. He quickly fell behind the others, who were still jogging up ahead. He was impressed that Patricia could keep up with Jim. He was struggling just to keep them in sight.

So much for sticking together. Like it or not, they were about to get separated in the darkness.

Then a slight wind began to howl over the top of the mesa just as Fernando hit a patch of loose rocks. Losing his balance, he pitched forward on his hands and knees and cursed his two companions for leaving him behind. He picked himself up and searched for his flashlight, which he had dropped in the fall. The flashlight seemed to have disappeared into thin air, its beam of light extinguished.

When he did find the flashlight, a few minutes later, he discovered what he feared most: the damned thing had stopped working. So now he found himself all alone on the dark mesa, feeling abandoned and more than a little worried because in the fall he seemed to have lost the trail. The trail was poorly marked to begin with, having few cairns and trail signs. In the dark it was impossible to distinguish trail from mesa.

He began walking more slowly to avoid another mishap. When he came to a flat ridge, he decided to stop there and search for the trail. He found a boulder to use as a point of reference, and walked around it in an ever-widening circle but still found no evidence of the trail. There wasn't a trail marker in sight.

He considered his options and quickly decided the only real option was to head back down. He hadn't lost sight of the lights in the canyon below, so even without the trail he could make his way back down the mesa to Casa Rinconada and wait for the others. There was nothing else he could do at this point.

While he made his decision, he heard movement up ahead of him. Something was coming toward him in the darkness. He heard the crunching of rocks and felt the air currents shift around him. Now the sound multiplied until it seemed to be coming at him from all directions. Suddenly he saw them, dark shadows moving out of the darkness into the pale moonlight, huge beasts whose eyes seem to glow in the dark, reflecting the light of the moon.

Then they stopped, just as suddenly, and he realized he was looking at a herd of animals, deer or more likely elk since they were huge, as large or larger than a full-grown cow. The beasts stared at him, as surprised to see him as he was to see them. A stand-off.

"Sorry," he said, realizing as he said it how ridiculous this sounded. He waved and made his way slowly toward the still motionless herd of elk, not knowing if elk could be dangerous to humans. He had never bumped into a herd of wild elk under these or any other circumstances, so how the hell would he know? That's all he needed, to be attacked by an angry elk in the dark. Wouldn't Antonio and Manny love to rib him about that? He would never hear the end of it.

So he moved gingerly through the herd, as he'd been taught to do around other animals. Who knew what elk were capable of? For all he knew one of the big bull elks could take exception to his presence and send him flying off the mesa with one powerful head butt. Fortunately, the herd parted to accommodate him as he began his descent, moving slowly down off the mesa without the aid of a flashlight.

He came across what he thought was the trail near the bottom and followed it around the base of the cliff to Casa Rinconada. There he took a seat on a nearby bench and waited for Jim and Patricia to return. He waited almost an hour before he heard them coming down the trail talking in subdued tones. By the sound of their voices he could tell they were discouraged.

"We never caught up with them, whoever it was," Jim said, walking up to the Great kiva. "They disappeared down one of the man-made stairways into South Gap and then put out or turned off the light."

"South Gap?" Fernando asked.

"That's the valley between South and West mesas. It's where the south entrance to the canyon comes in."

All this was news to him. "So there's a road coming in from the south?"

"Yes, a county road, but it's very primitive, much worse than the road coming in from the north. You need a four-wheel drive."

"So someone with a four-wheel drive could come in from the south and not be noticed?"

"Well, not really," Jim said. "The road comes into the canyon and connects with the Chaco Loop, which is gated, so it doesn't provide direct access to the ruins, if that's what you mean."

Fernando nodded, pondering the possibilities.

"By the way, what happened to you?" Patricia asked him.

"I couldn't keep up, and then my flashlight stopped working and I ran into a heard of what looked like elk, so I turned around and came back here to wait for you. Nothing I could do."

"Yes, there's a herd of Elk living on South Mesa, about twenty of them," Jim said. "They come down in the evening to graze along Chaco Wash."

"That explains it," Fernando said.

Jim looked around. "Well, it's late, we need to get back so we can get some sleep. There's nothing more we can do tonight."

"Good. My legs feel like rubber," Patricia said.

Jim grabbed the two reflecting mirrors he'd removed from the kiva and then led the way back down the trail to the parking lot, with him and Patricia following behind. Jim tossed the mirrors in the back of the jeep and climbed into the front seat.

Fernando squeezed into the rear seat and once again let Patricia ride shotgun.

Before starting the jeep, Jim turned to Patricia and asked, "Are you okay? You seem kind of subdued."

She shrugged. "Well, I'm not real happy about being here. You probably know the Navajo have a lot of superstitions about this place. Lots of people love Chaco and think it's a holy place of peace or whatever, but we think of it as a place where bad things happened. Very bad things."

"You mean the 'Gambler's Tale'?"

"That and other legends of the 'White Place' where bad things happened. Where a tyrannical ruler did bad things to his people. Tortured and destroyed them."

"I remember," Jim said.

"My father and his father both tended their goat herds on Chacra Mesa," Patricia continued. "Neither of them would ever set foot in the canyon itself. Too many bad spirits, they said. A dangerous place."

"Do they still feel that way?" Jim asked.

"The Navajo? Yes, my father does, anyway. There's a photo I've seen that captures the ghosts. It's titled 'The Ghosts of Pueblo Bonito' and shows ghosts hovering over Bonito, a swarm of white ghosts. You can find it on a Facebook page called 'Southwest Images.' I can't remember the name of the photographer, but the photo is only a few years old. So they're still here, the ghosts."

On their way out Jim stopped to lock the exit gate and they drove back to the staff barracks in silence.

7

Fernando woke up on a strange sofa thinking he was in some sort of torture chamber. Then he remembered. He and Patricia had driven to Chaco Canyon yesterday afternoon to investigate the murder of Pete Chavez, one of the park rangers. They'd ended up staying the night in the staff barracks, Patricia with Betty Madsen and him with Jim Murphy. That was the reason he found himself lying face down on a lumpy sofa in a world of pain.

Now he heard noises coming from the kitchen and smelled freshly brewed coffee, enticing him to get up and face the day as only the aroma of fresh coffee could. But when he tried to move, his back and shoulders began to bark. Cramps everywhere, some in parts of his anatomy that he never knew existed. He was definitely too old and set in his ways to sleep on a sagging sofa in a military style barracks. He needed the comforts of his own soft bed.

"Coffee's ready, if you're awake," Jim said from the kitchen, standing over the coffee machine.

Was he awake? Maybe this was all a bad dream, a nightmare. How had a detective from Santa Fe ended up sleeping on a sofa in Chaco Canyon?

"Coming." He managed to sit up, which was a little more comfortable. He stretched his arms over his head. "What time is it?"

"Six a.m. sharp," Jim said, a tall beanpole of a man with thinning blond hair and bright blue eyes. "We do the morning check at seven, right before we open the gates. You and Patricia can come along this morning. I'll show you the digging at Pueblo Bonito."

Jim talked fast, too fast for six a.m.

Fernando stood up, rubbing the small of his back with both hands. The kitchen and living area occupied one large room, with a small table next to a window in front where Jim was sitting, drinking his coffee and eating his breakfast. Jim looked to be in his mid thirties, with way too much energy for this early in the morning.

"Help yourself. There's oatmeal in the pot, fruit and nuts on the counter. I don't have time for much of a breakfast out here. Got to get a fast start on the day so we can get the visitor center open at seven."

He grunted. "I'm going to need a lot of coffee before I can even think about eating."

Jim laughed. "You'll wake up as soon as we get outside in the fresh air. To me Chaco is a special place, in spite of what Patricia said last night. I love the place."

"I can tell."

"Yeah, I grew up in Grand Junction, hiking and skiing on Colorado's West Range. My parents took me to Mesa Verde when I was ten. I fell in love with the idea of working at a national park as a ranger. And here I am."

Fernando nodded.

"You've been here before, right?" Jim asked.

"Only once...before I was married. Camped here with a couple of friends one summer. Hotter than hell, as I recall. To make matters worse, we drank too much beer and got seriously dehydrated."

"Hah!" Jim laughed again.

After a cup of coffee, Fernando went into the bathroom and splashed water on his face, washing away yesterday's sweat. He didn't take time to change clothes. Why bother? He would just get them dirty.

He managed to eat a few pieces of fruit before they left. The coagulated oatmeal was more than he could stomach. Ranger Jim waited impatiently while he drank another cup of coffee to wash down the fruit. He admired Jim's good-natured enthusiasm. It was an admirable quality, one that he lacked.

"Okay, let's go pick up Patricia."

He buckled on his holster and followed Jim outside to the staff jeep.

They found Patricia sitting on the porch chair outside the end unit waiting for them. Another fast starter. He climbed in back so she could ride shotgun.

"Morning, Ms. Begay," Jim said, ever chipper.

She returned the greeting and asked him to call her Patricia.

"Okay, Patricia and Fernando, let me show you what we do every morning."

Jim gunned the jeep and drove onto the Chaco Loop to the

locked gate near the visitor center. There he jumped out and unlocked the gate and pulled it back toward the ditch. Then he jumped back in and took off in a cloud of dust toward the ruins. They passed the Una Vida and Hungo Pavi Great Houses and then slowed down as they approached the Pueblo Bonito parking lot.

After he cut the ignition Jim turned to them. "Let me give you the lay of the land. This is considered 'Downtown Chaco' because the two largest ruins in the canyon are side by side. Pueblo Bonito here and over there Chetro Ketl."

Fernando remembered his one camping trip to Chaco back in the 1970s. He especially remembered visiting the massive 650-room Pueblo Bonito, the center of power during the Chacoan empire that lasted from about 850 to 1150 A.D. Back then Chaco was an urban metropolis that attracted traders and religious pilgrims from as far away as California and down in Mesoamerica. What happened to end the Chacoan empire was something of a mystery. Most experts blamed drought, famine, social unrest, and intertribal warfare, as he recalled. The usual suspects.

"Until now the looters have left Bonito and Chetro Ketl alone because they've been more thoroughly excavated than the other ruins," Jim said.

Fernando interrupted Jim. "Do you check all the ruins every day?"

"No, we don't have the staff to do that. We do a drive-by of the ruins inside the canyon every day, morning and evening, but the Great Houses on top of the mesas are difficult for us to monitor. The only access is by foot on trails that range from four to ten miles round-trip, and all of them involve steep climbing, which takes a lot more time. You can't just drive by and take a look. We send someone up on North Mesa every two weeks or so, but West and South mesas are pretty much left alone, by necessity. We just don't have the staff to get up there."

Jim shook his head. "Don't get me wrong, if we happen to see lights or unusual activity up on one of the mesas, then we'll check it out."

Fernando looked puzzled. "What do you mean by lights and unusual activity?"

"Well—" Jim started, and then trailed off. "Let me choose my words carefully. I don't mean looters. What I mean is that it's not all that uncommon for us to see lights moving among the ruins or to hear sounds coming from different parts of the canyon. Like chanting,

I guess, would be the best way to explain it. We almost never find anything, no source for the lights or the sounds. Some things are best left alone, I suppose. Maybe it's better not to know."

"Ghosts," Patricia said quietly. "The ghosts are everywhere here. I can feel them."

Jim's smile disappeared quickly. It was as though she had said something forbidden.

"I'm from Tsaya, just a few miles west of the canyon." She waved her hand in a semi circle. "All the land surrounding this canyon is Navajo land. We've known about the ghosts for a long time."

Fernando broke the silence. "Ghosts...and now looters."

"Well, let me show you where Pete was killed." Jim jumped out of the jeep, heading toward Bonito. He moved quickly, like a jackrabbit. He and Patricia followed along behind.

They walked down the trail to Bonito. The Great House seemed to rise up out of the canyon floor, its red sandstone walls jagged silhouettes against a deep blue sky. They stepped through a doorway into an open plaza and followed the north-south wall that split the ruin in half. Toward the rear of Bonito they came to a series of small rooms linked by T-shaped doors. Jim stopped and pointed toward the bottom of a stairway.

"We found Pete's body right here, you can still see the dried blood. He left his jeep in the parking lot and walked down here to confront the looters. He had no way to protect himself, nothing. When I got here, after he didn't return at the usual time, he was already dead. I tried but couldn't find a pulse. I radioed the visitor center, and Leroy called Cuba for an ambulance."

Fernando looked around the area. "You said he was beaten with a shovel you found nearby?"

"That's what the deputy thought, anyway. His face was disfigured. It was a bloody mess. And there was blood on the shovel."

"Why do you say the deputy thought? Do you have a different explanation?"

"No, only that his head was twisted at a weird angle on his shoulders. It looked like his neck was broken."

Fernando remembered the body of Tom Flynn back in Santa Fe. His neck had been snapped in much the same way.

"Anyway, the digging is in the next room."

Jim walked down the stairway and around to a T-shaped doorway. When he poked his head through the doorway he stopped.

"Oh shit! Look at this damage. They were digging again last

night. The goddamned mirrors were a ruse to keep us out of the way. I should have known. Fuck me!"

Fernando and Patricia came down to take a look.

"The bastards destroy everything they dig up because they're not careful. Just look!"

They examined fist-sized pieces of broken pottery and smaller shards scattered everywhere. In one deep pit they found something much more troubling: human bones. They saw what looked like a leg bone and several ribs, some of them shattered by a shovel or pick axe.

"These will have to be reburied," Jim said, shaking his head gravely. "I'll have to call the state Cultural Affairs Department when we get back to the visitor center and report the violation."

"Will you rebury them here?" Fernando asked.

"We have to. We have to follow NAGPRA guidelines. You know, the Native American Graves Protection and Repatriation Act."

Patricia remained silent, staring at the bones.

Jim turned to them. "So what can we do to stop these people?

"We need a plan," Fernando said. "Maybe we could spend the night in the ruin waiting for them...or come early in the morning while it's still dark."

"I vote for the second option," Patricia said. "I don't know about you, but I'm not spending the night in an ancestral ruin inhabited by ghosts. No way."

They watched her walk off toward Kin Kletso, about a hundred yards west of Bonito.

"Tomorrow morning, then," Jim said. "Before the crack of dawn, while it's still dark."

Jim stood back and let Fernando examine the digging. The looters had dug multiple holes in the hard-packed earth, not bothering to replace the dirt. It was a hurried, sloppy job. A three by three-foot section of the rear wall had been busted out with a heavy instrument.

"This room was part of Wetherill's trading post, which was built outside against the rear wall. Here, let me show you."

Jim led him back up the stairway and around to a rear exit. They walked along the rear wall of the Great House until they came to the section that had been broken through.

"Right here where we're standing was the main part of the trading post. You can see the different rock layers that mark the doorway into Bonito that Wetherill added. The Park Service patched the doorway many years ago."

Fernando nodded. "So... according to the Flynn Journal this is where Wetherill would have buried the artifacts he wanted to hide. Somewhere in these rooms or outside near the rear wall."

Jim checked his watch. "The visitors will start arriving any minute now. I need to close off this area around the rear wall and the room inside."

He waited while Jim walked back to the jeep. He returned with a roll of yellow 'Caution' tape and an armful of wooden stakes. He staked off the area around the broken section of wall and then did the same for the room inside the ruin, where most of the digging had occurred.

Finished, they walked around to the front of Bonito where Patricia waited for them. Murphy pointed to the west. "If you look over there, you'll see a little fenced plot. That's where Wetherill and his wife Marietta are buried. She died in nineteen fifty-three, forty-three years after his murder."

"More ghosts," Patricia said.

They walked down to the parking lot. Before leaving, Jim pointed to an outcropping of cliff further down the trail west of Kin Kletso. "That's where Wetherill was murdered."

"For looting?" Fernando asked.

"No, I don't think so. It was apparently a dispute over a stolen horse that was mistreated, or at least that was the official explanation, though there are rumors of womanizing and bad blood and what have you. There was a lot of tension between Wetherill and the Navajo. Anyway, he was ambushed and killed right there by a man named Chis-Chilling-Begay."

Patricia froze. "No relation," she said. "Begay is the most common Navajo name."

"Sorry, I didn't mean to imply...." Jim said, but she was already climbing into the jeep.

8

After Jim unlocked and opened the exit gate, he dropped them off at the staff barracks and then headed for the visitor center to report for work. By now the sun had climbed over the canyon wall and flooded the canyon with light. The warm sunlight made his back feel better and gave him hope that he could survive what looked to be a long, hot day at Chaco Canyon.

"What's next?" Patricia asked.

"I'd like to check out the campground, see if there are any obvious suspects running around with picks and shovels," Fernando said. "Wouldn't it be nice if it were that easy. Then we should probably check out some of the other ruins, see if anyone's been digging elsewhere."

With that, they climbed into the cruiser and drove up to the campground. They parked next to the ranger station, a trailer, where Betty had the day's campground duty. She waved from up the road where she was checking the campsites one by one, clipboard in hand.

"Greetings," she said, a short woman with gray hair and glasses. "What can I do for you?"

"Have you noticed any suspicious activity at the campground?" he asked. "Anyone who's here with more tools than camping equipment?"

"Well, like I told Patricia this morning, it's really hard for me to imagine how our campers could be digging in the ruins. I mean, the gates are locked at sunset, and we monitor their comings and goings. They couldn't possibly be digging in the daylight, and I just don't see how they could get into the park after dark without us noticing them."

Betty looked around the campground, thinking.

"That said, you might check out the guy at site forty. He slept in the bed of his pickup last night and didn't bring much camping equipment. And there are a couple of old hippies in the turquoise van at site thirty-five. You might take a look at their van. They don't seem to do much, just sit around smoking weed. But again, I just don't see how campers could get access to the ruins at night."

"Isn't there another road into Chaco from the north? When I camped here back in the seventies, I remember entering on a completely different road. You came down a steep incline into the canyon, with a small ruin off to the right just as you reached the bottom. Not the current paved road to the visitor center."

"That was the old Highway Fifty-seven from Nageezi," she said. "It hasn't been used as an entrance to the canyon for at least twenty years. You can still take it part way on North Mesa but not all the way into the canyon. And even on North Mesa it's rough going because the county stopped maintaining it years ago."

"We should check it out anyway," Patricia added.

"Suit yourself."

After Betty excused herself, Fernando and Patricia walked through the tent circle to site 40, nestled between two boulders jutting out from the side of the box canyon. They looked for the guy who slept in the bed of his pickup, which happened to be parked in front of the boulders blocking their view of the campsite. He noticed a large steel toolbox in the bed of the pickup alongside a sleeping bag and a small cooler. When they walked around the pickup, they found him sitting at the picnic table drinking a can of beer and watching them approach.

Having a beer this early in the morning seemed odd to him, but then he remembered his first trip to Chaco as a young man. He and his camping buddies had done much the same.

"Morning," Fernando said. "We're checking all the campsites for illegal digging. Do you mind if we take a look in your tool box?"

"What's that got to do with me?" he said, setting down his can of beer and walking over to the pickup, a big man with a full black beard and muscles bulging under his T-shirt. "Are you accusing me?"

Fernando backed away. The man could be dangerous.

Seeing the problem, Patricia walked over and flashed her badge. "FBI. You can either show us what's in your toolbox, or I can go down to the visitor center right now and have the FBI run your name and license through our system. It's your choice. What'll it be?"

The big man glared at Patricia, then said, "Knock yourself out!" He took a key out of his pocket, unlocked the padlock, and threw open the lid of the toolbox. Inside were mostly power tools, but there were also extension cords and a variety of hand tools. No shovel or pick.

"I've been working construction in Farmington," he said. "I'm on my way back to Santa Fe."

Fernando nodded. "Okay, sorry for the bother."

He followed Patricia to Campsite 35, where a couple of old hippies were camping, according to Betty. The site sat back from the road near the canyon wall partly hidden from view. Their turquoise van, on the other hand, remained in full view, as conspicuous as a pink flamingo in a row of pigeons. Stickers cluttered the rear of the van: 'Free Tibet,' 'Save the Planet,' and assorted marijuana images of various sizes and shapes. Could they be any more conspicuous?

He headed for the tent near the canyon wall while Patricia inspected the van. Walking through a clump of sagebrush, he saw a camping stove and assorted gear piled on the picnic table and a couple of folding chairs set up by the fire grate. Getting closer, he caught a glimpse of someone poking a head out of the tent opening and then a blur that looked like that someone dashing out of the tent and running toward the canyon wall. Running!

He hurried to the tent and called out, "Who's there? Police!"

"Yesssss," came a woman's voice from inside the tent. Seconds later she unzipped the tent door and tentatively poked her head outside, looking up at him with squinting eyes, an elderly woman with white hair and a deeply wrinkled face. She smiled.

"Who ran out of your tent a minute ago?"

"Oh, well, it must have been my husband. I don't think I've seen anyone else in here." She turned and looked behind her.

He couldn't tell if she was being sarcastic, or if she was stoned out of her mind on pot.

"Please step out of the tent, ma'am," Fernando said.

"Okay, but I have to warn you, I have balance issues," she said, and grabbed hold of his arm as she stepped out. He helped her over to the picnic table, where she sat down and looked up at him bemused.

"I was just meditating before you came," she said in a sweet sing-song kind of voice.

"So what are you and your husband doing at Chaco?"

"We're making a tour of holy places. I'm sure you know Chaco Canyon is a very holy place. It's the Center Place of the Pueblo people. We're going to Canyon de Chelly next and then to on Sedona. We live in Taos. Well, Arroyo Hondo anyway."

No surprise there, Fernando mused. Arroyo Hondo had been

famous for potheads since the days of Dennis Hopper back in the 1970s.

He looked around for the husband, the person who had bolted out of the tent. He figured the husband was probably looking for a place to hide his stash, since weed was still illegal in the state of New Mexico. He needn't have worried, though, because moments later he saw Patricia escorting the wayward husband back to the tent. The old man carried a leather satchel he had apparently tried to hide in the crevices along the cliff wall.

The animated little man chatted excitedly with Patricia, as if they were old friends, telling her they just loved traveling around to special places and enjoying the sites and the camping and, oh sure, they enjoyed a little recreational weed, which helped diminish the effects of dementia, you know, because it was a proven scientific fact that weed helped control epileptic seizures and all forms of dementia, including Alzheimer's and Parkinson's.

The old man held out his hand for him to shake, a spry little man, bald except for a few tufts of gray hair spiking out from his ears. He wore jeans and a faded turquoise T-shirt from the Indian Pueblo Cultural Center in Albuquerque that matched the color of their van.

After shaking hands, the husband introduced himself and his wife as Roy and Carla Tompkins from Arroyo Hondo. "We're Lawrentians. You know...D. H. Lawrence...who wrote *Lady Chatterley's Lover*?"

Yes, Fernando knew about D. H. Lawrence and *Lady Chatterley's Lover*, but he opted not to pursue the Lawrence reference and instead asked, "So what do you have in the bag there, Roy?"

"Just our medicinals," Carla added.

Patricia opened the satchel and showed him the contents: a bag of pot, rolling materials, and a couple of pipes.

Fernando shrugged. "You haven't been doing any digging in the canyon, have you?"

"Oh, no, we would never deface a holy place like Chaco," Carla said. "We would never be able to forgive ourselves. The spirits wouldn't approve."

"No, they wouldn't," Patricia said.

Fernando shook his head but said nothing.

Patricia walked back behind the turquoise van, where she motioned for him to join her. "What do you think? The van is clean."

"Let them be," he said. "Who cares about a couple ounces of pot. The state legislature is going to legalize marijuana soon anyway."

Patricia went back to the tent and handed the satchel to Roy. "Enjoy your camping. And your medicinals."

On their way back to the cruiser, they stopped at an empty campsite and sat down at the picnic table to make plans for the afternoon. They decided to stop first at the visitor center and call their respective offices to tell them they would be spending another night at Chaco. And he would call Estelle and try to defuse her expected reaction to his extended absence. Then they would do a walk-around of all the ruins inside the canyon in order to get their bearings. Last, they would accompany Jim on his nightly security check at sunset, looking for looters. If anyone attempted to dig in the canyon tonight, they would be ready.

First, though, they needed to stop at the visitor center and get some bottles of water. It was too damn hot to walk around Chaco without a supply of cold water.

9

Linda laughed when she heard Fernando's voice. "Chief wants to know what the hell you're doing at Chaco and when the hell you're coming back. Those are his exact words. Oh, wait. He also said, 'Tell Lopez he needs to put in for vacation time if he intends to fuck around Chaco Canyon all week.' That's a direct quote, Fernando. So what the hell ARE you doing at Chaco Canyon?"

"I'm investigating Pete Chavez's murder! Which is what the Chief sent me here to do, remember?"

Linda laughed.

"Tell him to fuck off," Fernando said, only partly joking. "No, seriously, tell him I need at least one more day. Looters are digging in the ruins at night, and one of them might be Luis Lujan of Santa Fe. He's the son of Tom Flynn's housekeeper, the woman who found Flynn's body. So far we have no leads on who killed our friend Pete Chavez."

Linda sighed. "Okay, I'll tell him, but he won't be a happy man."

"Yeah, what else is new?"

His relations with the Chief had been strained since the day Stuart, an Anglo, was hired. The bad blood between them never seemed to end. As a consequence Fernando had a reputation for being prickly. But who wouldn't be prickly after watching one Anglo after another being promoted ahead of him. It took him twenty years to make detective. Compare that to the three years it took the Chief's nephew to make detective. What a joke! Dickless Andy as the other cops called him had the lightest workload of any of them.

When he first joined the department thirty years ago he and the other young Chicano cops were treated like second-class citizens. Ironic, since he and many of the others were from Santa Fe's oldest families. Their treatment was especially galling to Fernando because his mother was Anglo and so he had always resisted ethnic tribalism. But he learned to swallow his pride and hold his tongue. He learned to accept the shit assignments. He paid his dues. Big time.

But he hadn't forgotten. Nor had he forgiven.

Patricia had the opposite experience. Her office told her to take as much time as she needed. Any violation of the Antiquities Act was serious business to the FBI—if artifacts were actually removed or destroyed.

Hanging up the phone, Patricia shook her head and smiled. "They couldn't care less that I'm out of the office. I think they'd be happy if I never came back," she said laughing. "Except it's not really funny."

When they finished calling, they loaded a cooler with bottles of water. With the cooler in the trunk of the cruiser and a map of Chaco Canyon in the glove compartment they drove to the end of the Chaco Loop and parked in the Pueblo del Arroyo Parking Lot. He checked out Pueblo del Arroyo, while Patricia walked through Kin Kletso, the small ruin just west of Pueblo Bonito. Behind Kin Kletso an ancient stairway climbed to the top of North Mesa, where a web of Chacoan roads extended out in all directions.

He saw no evidence of digging in Pueblo del Arroyo, so he decided to join Patricia at Kin Kletso. He stepped around the metal gate blocking the former entrance to the canyon from Highway 57 and walked along the old road now overgrown with weeds. According to the map Jim had given them, this section of the road dated from the 1890s when Richard Wetherill operated his trading post at Pueblo Bonito and used the road to move goods in and out of the canyon. The road branched off beyond West Mesa. One branch extended due west all the way to the Chuska Mountains near the Arizona state line, while another branch circled around North Mesa toward Highway 550 and Nageezi.

Just beyond Kin Kletso Patricia pointed to a set of tire tracks in the sand. "These tracks are fresh. And look, they stop right here. They don't continue on past the gate. They come in from the west and stop here at Kin Kletso, an easy walk over to Pueblo Bonito. So whoever's doing the digging is coming down through the Navajo Reservation, from the west or maybe the north. That's why the rangers don't see them at the campground or the visitor center."

She was right, Fernando realized. That explained a lot of things. "Okay, then let's follow the road a ways, see what we find."

She nodded.

They started hiking down the road, which ran straight for a couple of hundred yards. As they approached the spot where Richard Wetherill was murdered, Patricia left the road and walked down the bank into Chaco Wash and around. He had no idea what she was doing until it occurred to him that she was trying to avoid the area. He said nothing. She rejoined him farther down where the road circled to the right around a box canyon, with another small ruin, Casa Chiquita, visible on the opposite side of the canyon.

Fernando stopped when he saw the box canyon, pointing to the canyon rim and the faint ribbon of a ledge that ran along the cliff down into the canyon.

"That's where the old Highway 57 came into the canyon, right there. I remember driving down the incline when I camped here. You can still see the line of the road. And that's the small ruin I remembered, Casa Chiquita. It was the first thing you saw when you entered the canyon."

Patricia studied what was left of the road. None of the tire tracks went up the incline, which was understandable given that rockslides and erosion had damaged the road beyond repair. It would be virtually impassible for vehicles, even four wheel drive vehicles, but not for foot traffic. She called his attention to footprints going up and down the road.

"Let's check it out," she said.

So he led the way up the steep climb, hiking around deep ruts and fallen rocks. Patricia passed him halfway up the incline. By the time they came to the top of North Mesa he was out of breath. He was envious of her youth and her stamina, but he reminded himself that she was a good twenty years younger. What the hell did he expect?

The road flattened out on top, which made walking a lot easier. The view opened up on a vast expanse of high desert terrain of ridges and rock formations, dotted by dark clumps of sage and rabbit bush. In the distance a few cattle and sheep grazed on the sparse vegetation. They followed the footprints for over a mile with the rising sun getting hotter overhead. He wished they'd remembered to bring a couple of water bottles with them. He made a mental note to borrow a backpack from Jim so he could carry the bottles when hiking.

Up ahead they eventually came to what looked like a small parking lot or pull-off along what was left of the road. Coming closer, they realized they had come across a much-used campsite, with a fire pit and stone circle in the center. Around the blackened stones several five-gallon cans had been overturned and placed around the fire pit to be used for seating.

The area surrounding the pit was littered with garbage of one kind or another, cans and bottles as well as paper and plastic wrappers caught in the bushes and flapping in the breeze. There were multiple tire tracks leading up to the campsite, but only footprints from the campsite into the canyon itself. Some of the people who used this area were walking into the canyon.

Without speaking, they entered the campsite and started to look around. The fire pit didn't look like it had been used in the last twenty-four hours. The cans and bottles were mostly beer and hard liquor containers.

He kicked one of the beer cans.

"Looters could use this place as a staging area," Patricia said.

Suddenly from the west they heard someone shouting at them.

"What's that?" he asked, pointing to a man standing next to an ATV about a hundred yards away. He was holding what looked like a rifle in his hands and shouting at them. He sounded angry.

Suddenly a shot rang out!

"He's shooting at us, get down!" Fernando shouted.

And then a second shot.

Fernando squatted low in the sand and took his service revolver out of its holster.

Patricia, lying on her stomach, grabbed his arm. "The shots were fired over our heads. Wait."

While they watched, the man climbed into his All Terrain Vehicle and headed their way. He maneuvered the ATV around the larger bushes and across a dry arroyo bed, finally pulling up in the middle of the road. He jumped out, rifle in hand, walking slowly, carefully toward the two crouching figures, not knowing what to expect from the intruders.

"Oh," the man said when he came close enough to get a good look at Patricia. He said something in Navajo.

Patricia stood up and dusted off her clothing.

Their visitor nodded, a Navajo with short-cropped black hair wearing a western hat, jeans and a white T-shirt. He had turquoise bracelets on both arms and a beaded belt tied around his waist. He lowered his rifle and then stopped a moment to pull up his sagging jeans.

"Sorry," he said. "I thought you were looters or hippies...or maybe guys from the oil rigs who come here to get drunk. They think just because their companies lease from the BLM they can do what they want on Navajo land. This is our land. They have no business here."

"That's why we're here," Patricia said. "I'm an FBI agent and my partner here is a detective from the Santa Fe Police Department. We've come to investigate illegal digging in the canyon."

"Ben Yazzie," the man introduced himself, coming over to join them near the fire pit.

Yazzie continued. "Yeah, they come in here from the oil rigs to party and get drunk. Last week coupla guys came in with two Navajo women I hadn't seen before. Don't know who they were, where they come from, but all four of them were intoxicated and messing around, you know, making a lot of noise and yelling. I came down and told them to get off the reservation and they threatened me with a gun. They pointed a gun at me and told me to get lost or they would kill me. So that's why I'm carrying my gun today. I got to protect myself. These are bad people."

Fernando and Patricia introduced themselves properly.

Yazzie motioned to the west. "That's my hogan and my corral up there on the ridge. And those are my goats and my cattle. This is all Navajo land, as far as you can see on the mesa."

Fernando nodded. "Have you noticed anyone camping up here recently? Here or elsewhere along the road?"

"Yeah, a coupla guys camped here the other night. They didn't make any noise, so I left them alone."

"What about the canyon? Have you seen anyone digging in the ruins?"

"No, I don't go into the canyon much," Yazzie said. "I stay away from that place. But I see them up here all the time. They throw their trash everywhere. Look at the mess they leave behind. Used to be, I would come down and try to pick up their mess, but no more. I can't keep up with it."

"Bastards!" Patricia said.

"Yeah, they're bad people," Yazzie said. "Come to think of it, I have seen a coupla ATVs recently, coming in and out of the canyon. I think it was two different ATVs. Maybe the same one."

"Were they looters?" Fernando asked. "Taking artifacts out of the canyon?"

"Maybe. I can't say for sure, but I wouldn't doubt it. My wife's family lives down by Pueblo Pintado, southeast of here, and man, you should see that ruin. The looters have picked the place clean. Nothing left but the holes in the ground where they've dug."

"Well, if they do come back, or if you see someone you think is digging in the canyon, you might go down to the visitors center and tell the rangers," he said. "They would call the San Juan County Sheriff or the FBI, depending. With a little luck we may be able to catch the looters before all the ruins in the canyon look like Pueblo Pintado. Or worse!"

"Like I said, I don't go into the canyon much. But I might go up to Nageezi and call the sheriff. Problem is, sometimes they don't pay any attention to us when we call. They tell us to call the Tribal Police or the BLM, you know. But yeah, I'll do what I can."

So they left it at that. Ben Yazzie would do what he could.

Yazzie raised his hand to hold them a moment longer. "And be careful, bad things happen here, always have. It might be worse than ever today, I don't know. Lotta bad people coming here now, lotta bad people everywhere."

After Yazzie climbed aboard his ATV and drove off, he and Patricia began the long walk back, retracing their steps to Kin Kletso and the Pueblo del Arroyo parking lot.

"What now?" she asked.

"How about a nap?"

She laughed. "How old did you say you were?"

"Too old for this."

She smiled. "And yet, here you are."

He was starting to like Patricia Begay. They'd come a long way since that awkward drive from Albuquerque to Chaco.

10

After closing the visitor center and locking the entry and exit gates, the park rangers had agreed to meet in Jim's unit to share information and to discuss how they should approach their new, dangerous situation. Betty and Leroy Roybal arrived first. Only Chet Morris had been unable to come because he had this evening's campground duty. They began the meeting with a moment's silence for their fallen colleague, Pete Chavez.

Jim took the opportunity to introduce Fernando and Patricia to Leroy, who hadn't yet met them. Then he addressed the group.

"Here's what we know so far," Jim said. "We think the people digging at Bonito are coming in at night on the old wagon road, from the west, which is why the gates haven't kept them out and why we haven't spotted them at the campground. We think they're using small four-wheel drive vehicles, maybe ATVs. We don't know what they've taken out of the park so far, if anything, but we expect them to be back for more, probably tonight. Has anyone else seen any other suspicious activity?

Betty raised her hand from a rocking chair across the room. "Yeah, I caught Roy and Carla, our two old hippie campers at site thirty-five, trying to deposit the cremated remains of Carla's mother in the cave up on Chaco Canyon Overlook," she said and then turned to Fernando and Patricia on the sofa. "That's the trail right off the campground. They were smoking pot and reciting some New Age mumbo-jumbo about helping or guiding her mother into the spirit world."

Everyone laughed but Jim. "Sounds amusing, but it's really not. Bringing human remains into the park is strictly forbidden, because it can screw up any future DNA analyses researchers might perform on remains found in the canyon. We get this all the time, though.

Pueblo Bonito and Casa Rinconada are the most popular repositories, although Chetro Ketl has seen its share of dumping. People even try to scatter the ashes of their pets. Can you imagine? Bringing Fido's ashes all the way to Chaco for dispersal?"

"Woof!" Leroy joked.

Even Jim had to laugh at this.

Then Leroy raised his hand, sitting next to Patricia.

"This isn't about looting, or scattering human ashes, but I think we may be in for trouble with the new campers at sites thirty-four and eighteen. I think it's a single woman named Marcy in the tent at site thirty-four and a couple, the Bryans, in the RV at site eighteen. Must be in their late thirties or early forties, from their looks. Anyway, they hang around Marcy's tent nearly naked and have sex with each other at all hours of the day and night, all three of them. Some sort of kinky sex triangle. Already we've received three complaints about their lewd behavior."

Leroy had everyone's attention now.

"This afternoon an elderly woman from one of the RVs was walking through the tent circle and heard them going at it," Leroy continued. "She came up to me at the station and said, 'Sir, do you realize the people in the blue tent over there are copulating! At this time of day!'"

Everyone laughed.

"So who are these people, these copulators?" Jim asked.

"They're a strange lot. Friendly, but strange. The Bryans, Paul and June, claim to own a New Age shop on Canyon Road in Santa Fe. Something called 'Essentia,' where they sell oils and potions for all kinds of things, including sex. Paul delighted in telling me about all the sexual toys they sell. Therapeutic sexual toys, he insisted. And they also claim to be collectors."

"Collectors of what?" Fernando interjected.

"Didn't exactly say. Paul mentioned old rugs and pots, but he didn't go into any detail. The odd thing, though, is that they hang around at Marcy's tent instead of their fancy RV. They have one of those sleek little Mercedes-Benz Sprinters, but every time I see them they're naked, or half naked, running through the bushes in the Tent Circle. Go figure."

Jim frowned, not happy. "Well, did you speak to them about the complaints we've received?"

"Briefly, but Marcy, the oldest of the two women, said, I quote: 'it's okay, honey, I'm a sex therapist.'"

"Do we have any regulations about sex or public orgies?" Betty asked. "You know, so we don't become a brothel or a nudist colony. Can you imagine the sunburns we'd have?"

Again, everyone laughed.

"Not that I know of," Jim said. "But after hearing this, maybe we should think about writing one and posting it on signs. Something like: *Keep Your Clothes On And Your Sex Private*!"

They swapped nudist jokes for a few minutes, and then when no one else had anything to report Jim passed around beers and declared it was social hour.

Fernando took the opportunity to ask a question he'd been pondering since he arrived at Chaco. "This is only the second time I've been in the canyon, but I have the same reaction I did the first time. After seeing the Great Houses and all the monumental architecture, I can't help but wonder, why did the Chacoans leave? Why did they abandon the canyon? It must have been more than just drought, the standard explanation. I mean, drought is endemic to the Southwest, the Chacoans had practiced dry farming for centuries."

Jim took a deep breath. "Well, there are lots of theories, most of them pointing to drought and lack of resources, as you say. There's also the theories that blame social upheaval and warfare. I don't know, but when you consider that the Chaco phenomenon began about eight hundred and fifty AD and lasted well over three hundred years, you have to wonder if it simply reached the end of its natural lifespan."

"Kind of like where we are now," Leroy added, laughing.

Jim ignored the comment. "Beginning about eleven thousand fifty the civilization just seemed to run out of steam. Building at Chaco slowed to a stop. The royal line of its rulers came to an end. We know this because we found the royal burial chamber, room thirty-three in Pueblo Bonito, where royalty with identical mitochondrial DNA were buried along with tons of precious items beginning about eight hundred fifty and ending about eleven thousand fifty. Think about it, how many so-called empires have lasted more than three hundred years? Look at Mexico or South America, even Europe. Only a select few have lasted longer than three hundred years. So, personally, I just think Chaco may have reached the end of its natural life."

Jim turned to Patricia. "What do you think, Patricia?"

She paused for a moment. "Well, I think the Navajo and the Pueblo people are very similar. We each have our own migration story—or stories, since we are many different groups. I think Chaco may have been a way-station for the Pueblo people, not their Center

Place. The Hopi and Zuni and Acoma and Laguna moved on from here, and so did other groups. All of them found their own center places elsewhere. That's what I think."

"Way-station, I like that," Betty said. "It seems right."

"And by the time my people arrived in the Four Corners area in the fourteenth or fifteenth century, depending on which story you believe, only small groups of people were living in Chaco," Patricia continued. "Not the original Chacoans, but isolated groups of migrants traveling down from Mesa Verde and southern Colorado. Scavengers mostly. We have stories about the bad things that happened here, that drove the people away and kept them away. Kinda like the bad things that are still happening here, I guess."

After a moment of silence, Jim said, "Now that we solved the Chaco mystery, does anyone want another beer?"

They all raised their hands.

11

Just after midnight, as planned, Fernando and Patricia drove off in the staff jeep with Jim to confront the looters if they returned to Pueblo Bonito that night. The moon was still nearly full, so that Jim could drive without lights to take advantage of the element of surprise. When they came to the locked gate, he jumped out of his jeep and walked over to open the gate. He leaned over the gate, fumbling with something. Then he threw up his hands and started cursing. At first they thought he was having a problem getting the lock to open, but he came back and kicked at the jeep's front tire.

"You won't believe this. I don't believe it myself. Some asshole has chained the gate closed with a heavy gauge chain, the kind you use to pull Mack trucks out of the ditch."

"You're right, I don't believe it," Fernando said.

Jim didn't waste any more time. He jumped back in the jeep and gunned the engine, quickly driving up to the exit gate on the Chaco Loop. Once again he came back to the jeep cursing.

"Same thing. We won't be able to open tomorrow unless we can cut through the fucking chains. We don't have anything here that would cut through chains that big. Which means we'll have to call Cuba tomorrow morning to get a welder or someone with an industrial chain cutter. Fuck!"

"What about tonight?" Fernando asked. "They must be digging tonight, if they went to this much trouble."

"Our only option is to walk. Wait. Chet and Leroy both have bicycles. We can take the bikes, two of us anyway."

"Not me," Patricia said. "No way I'm going to ride a bicycle through the ruins at midnight."

Jim turned to him. "Are you game?"

"Hah! I haven't ridden a bicycle in years, but I'll give it a try."

Excited now, Jim spun the jeep around and raced down to the staff barracks, where he dropped off Patricia at Betty's unit. He didn't bother to ask Chet and Leroy if he could borrow their bicycles. Instead, he parked in front of the storage shed in back of the barracks and retrieved the two bicycles, checked their tires for air, and gave one to Fernando.

"You know how to operate a ten-speed, right?" Jim asked.

"I think I can manage."

"Then follow me, and remember, no lights, " Jim told him and pedaled off toward the gate.

Fernando followed at a safe distance, not wanting to chance a collision. At the locked gate they had to dismount and carry their bicycles around the steel frame. Once beyond the gate they pedaled off into the darkness.

He had never been fond of bicycles, partly because bicycle seats compressed his already enlarged prostate and made his groin ache, and partly because riding a bicycle exhausted him. Even worse, riding a bicycle in the dark was like committing suicide slowly. All the bumps and cracks in the pavement, the objects coming toward him in the dark that he could not recognize in the nick of time, all of them were trying to kill him. He was riding blindly to his own destruction like a damned fool.

He cursed the bicycle, he cursed Chaco Canyon, and he cursed himself for being stupid enough to come here in the first place.

The final insult was that Jim pedaled like a Lance Armstrong wannabe, much faster than he did, so there was absolutely no way he could keep up with him. By the time he pulled even with the Hungo Pavi ruin, halfway to Pueblo Bonito, he'd totally lost sight of Jim. He didn't foresee a problem, since they were both going to the same place, but as he approached Pueblo Bonito he began to hear sounds, someone talking and the clank of metal on rock.

He stopped pedaling and cruised for a few seconds so he could listen. Suddenly he heard someone cry out and the sound of a crash far ahead in the darkness. He didn't start to worry until he heard muffled and angry voices and the sound of a struggle.

He pedaled as fast as he could now. Off to his right he could make out the jagged walls of Chetro Ketl silhouetted against the North Mesa cliff. To his left he could see the luminous patch of sky over South Gap, between the shadows of West and South mesas. When the moon went behind a cloud he found himself riding into total darkness. He had to slow down because he could no longer see even the faint outline of the road.

The cloud had dispersed by the time he came to the massive Pueblo Bonito ruin, where shadows deepened into deeper shadows. He no longer heard the muffled voices, which worried him even more than hearing them earlier. He slowed to a crawl as he approached the parking lot, coasting the last twenty yards or so until he collided with the front wheel of Jim's bicycle.

Fernando fell sideways onto the pavement, yelping in spite of himself. He remained on the pavement for a few seconds, listening for any sound or movement. Nothing, so he got to his feet and quickly inspected Jim's bike. Its front wheel was bent out of shape as if Jim had either fallen or collided with something. But there was no sign of him anywhere.

He parked his bike against a road sign and began walking toward the Bonito ruin. When he came to the southern wall of the ruin he saw two dim lights over by Kin Kletso, growing fainter as they traveled west on the old wagon road toward the Highway 57 entrance that he and Patricia had inspected earlier that day. He checked the luminous dial on his watch. Nearly one thirty a.m. Whoever had come tonight had already finished digging and was now leaving. He cursed out loud. He was too late. He should have started earlier.

Then he remembered Jim. He needed to find Jim, who could be seriously injured or worse.

Fernando found a doorway into Bonito and stepped into the interior shadows. He stopped for a moment and let his eyes adjust. Then he walked along the north-south wall to the rear of the ruin. As he approached the stairway down into the rooms Jim had shown them he saw the looters had torn down the plastic 'Caution' tape and tossed it aside.

Moving slowly, he crept down the stairway into the darkness. He could make out evidence of new digging ahead. This morning's pits and trenches were deeper now, expanding. Fresh mounds of dirt blocked his way as he negotiated a path through the pits, which in the dark looked bottomless. He had no idea what if anything had been excavated, but he was certain of one thing: the fact that they kept coming back to dig meant they hadn't yet found Wetherill's artifacts.

"Jim?" he said quietly, not shouting because he didn't know for sure if all the looters had gone. He inspected the room as carefully as he could in the dark and then walked back outside and around the perimeter of the ruin to the rear wall. He examined the digging along the rear wall and the breach where the looters had busted through the rock. Then he walked along the wall, first to the west and then back to the east. He found nothing,

Fernando stopped to listen. The wind howled through the canyon sounding like a pack of far off wolves or maybe ghosts, as Patricia said. Chaco Canyon was now a city of ghosts.

He walked around to the front of the ruin and found another doorway. He stepped into the ruin, watching his step. In the moonlight the ruin looked dark and ominous, jagged black stone against a gray sky. The doorways to the subterranean rooms on the southeast side of the ruin were as black as ink. When he stepped down into the first suite of rooms it was like passing through a time-space portal into a different dimension, a different world. He could see nothing, not even where he was stepping.

"Jim?" he said again, a little louder than before. "Are you in here? Are you hurt? Let me help you."

Suddenly he heard a sound off to his left. Someone or something was moving in the darkness. Then came a crashing sound of falling rock, which spooked him. Losing his balance, he slipped on loose rock and stumbled sideways into a broken wall fragment. He grabbed ahold of the wall and used it to steady himself, listening for any further movement.

"Jim? Who's there?" he called out. He stopped to listen, but there was no answer, only the wind howling through the broken ruin. Feeling with his hands out in front of him as though he were blind, he made his way slowly toward the noise, not knowing what to expect.

Finally coming to an opening, possibly an ancient door, he stepped outside into the night. When he did, he spotted a shadow that looked human, a man wearing a long black coat and a wide-brimmed hat. The shrouded figure was directly ahead of him, gliding west along the base of North Mesa toward Kin Kletso. He was about to pursue the shadow, whatever it was, but by the time he reached the cliff, the shrouded figure had disappeared into the darkness. He waited and watched for a few minutes, but the figure did not reappear.

Uncertain about what to do next, Fernando walked back around to the parking lot. He found no sign of Jim anywhere and no evidence of a struggle. He began to wonder if Jim had been kidnapped. But why would the looters kidnap a park ranger? They were looters, not kidnappers.

What they wanted was the hidden artifacts, yes?

This is crazy, he said to himself. Think!

He returned to the fallen bicycle and then walked in ever widening circles around the parking lot. Nothing. So he walked down the short trail to Pueblo del Arroyo, the only Great House built in the center of the canyon next to Chaco Wash. Feeling uneasy, even dread, he walked into the maze of dark rooms, splashed by shadows cast by the moon. The sandstone walls seemed to bore in on him as though they were alive, huge animals moving in to devour him. His heart pounded.

He was suffocating!

Finally Fernando ran out of the dark ruin and yelled, "Jim?" Again, there was no response.

He could only assume the looters had kidnapped Jim. For ransom, or maybe to dispose of him somewhere out beyond West Mesa where no one would ever find his body. For all he knew, Jim could already be dead.

It was imperative he get back to staff barracks to tell the others what had happened. They would have to call the San Juan County Sheriff's Office and organize a search party at daybreak. They might have to close the park tomorrow to keep the hikers and campers out until the situation was sorted out. At the very least the park would have to remain closed until they could open the park gates, which entailed getting someone from Cuba to come out with a blow torch or an industrial chain cutter in order to cut the chains on the gates.

Fernando found his bicycle against the road sign where he had left it and again started pedaling, this time by his lonesome. His legs were cramping now, feeling as heavy as cement, but he pushed on, trying to ignore the pain. When he reached the barracks his legs were so stiff that he could hardly dismount, let alone walk.

He hobbled up to the barracks and started banging on all the doors one at a time. "Emergency! Wake up!"

Betty was the first to open her door, wearing a nightgown and robe. "What's the matter?" she asked, wiping the sleep from her eyes. Patricia stood behind her in pajamas.

"Jim's missing," Fernando said. "He may have been kidnapped."

"What? By whom?"

"By the looters! We were ambushed at the Bonito parking lot. He was riding ahead of me so I didn't see what happened. But I heard a crash and then voices and the sound of a struggle. I found his bicycle in the parking lot but no sign of Jim."

While they talked, Leroy staggered out of his door, shirt unbuttoned, trying to pull up his pants with one hand. He was carrying his shoes in his other hand. "What's this? Jim is missing?"

Fernando explained and then moved on to the last door, the unit inhabited by Chet Morris. He banged on the door, and when no one answered banged again. This time the door opened slowly, revealing Chet standing there in boxer shorts and nothing else. "Yeah?" Chet asked.

Jim had mentioned that Chet was something of a ladies man, and now Fernando saw why. Morris had a chiseled, handsome face with a sweep of blond hair falling across his eyes, beach boy style. He guessed Morris was no more than forty years old.

Walking up behind Morris was a skinny blond woman of about the same age, totally nude, all flopping tits and bush when she appeared at the door. With a big smile, she said, "My name's Marcy."

"Oh, yeah," Morris said. "This is Marcy. She's camping here with her friends, the Bryans. So what's up?"

Fernando explained the situation.

"Well, shit, what do we do now? You want to come in and talk?" Chet opened the door wide. Marcy made no effort to cover herself or to put on clothes. Instead, she stepped forward into the open doorway, in full resplendent view of everyone on the porch. Under the porch light she looked positively radiant, with a big friendly smile to match.

"I don't know if that's such a good idea," Fernando said, eyeing Marcy and her many attributes.

Betty and Patricia peered around him, staring at Marcy with a look of disapproval. He remembered what Betty had said about not wanting the campground to turn into a nudist colony. Looking at Marcy now, he realized she might not have been joking.

Leroy was still trying to button his shirt while ogling Marcy. The sight of a totally naked woman prancing around was not something you saw every day at staff barracks.

Someone needed to take charge here, so Fernando stepped up. "How about we meet at the visitor center tomorrow morning at six a.m. before you open," he said. "We can't do anything before then, anyway. We'll call the sheriff's office to report a missing person, and we'll call Cuba to get someone out here with a blowtorch so we can open the park gates."

Everyone agreed, so they dispersed to their respective units, Betty and Patricia still eyeing Marcy suspiciously, Leroy longingly. He checked his watch and groaned when he saw it was nearly three a.m.

He made his way into Jim's unit, ignoring the weird feeling of being there without his host, and plopped down on the sofa fully dressed, exhausted. He was so tired he didn't bother to grab a blanket or remove his shoes and socks.

Some time later a dull thumping on the wall woke him up, followed by the sound of Marcy screaming next door, "Oh, baby, yes, yes, fuck me!"

Cursing, he grabbed a sofa pillow and tried his best to smother himself.

12

Even the usually handsome Chet looked like damaged goods this morning: disheveled, unshaven, with dark bags under his eyes. None of the rest of them looked any better. They had gathered in the visitor center at six a.m. as promised, all of them dragging their bodies painfully through time and space. Fernando could barely walk, he was so sore from last night's ten-mile bicycle ride in the dark.

Fernando had called the San Juan County Sheriff's Office first thing, and one of the deputies was on his way to investigate Jim's disappearance. Betty had called a garage in Cuba, and they were sending out someone to cut the chains on the two gates so the park could be opened. The garage couldn't say when their employee would arrive since he had several calls already on his schedule and would have to take them first come, first serve. As a consequence they had no idea when they would be able to open the park to visitors.

"Can you friggin' believe it, this is a World Heritage Site!" Betty wailed. "You'd think we would be more important than changing a tire or towing some clown who broke down on Highway Five Fifty!"

"Isn't there a garage at Nageezi?' Fernando asked.

"Not with that kind of equipment," Leroy said.

Meanwhile, the parking lot out front of the visitor center had filled with vehicles waiting to enter the park. That included two tour buses. The complaining tourists were not a happy lot. Getting to Chaco was no easy task, and they resented having to wait on a hot concrete parking lot when they could be sightseeing and hiking, the reasons they had braved the long, rough drive.

So they had abandoned their vehicles and were gathering around the picnic tables out front or wandering down the trail to Una Vida, the nearest ruin to the visitor center. Every so often one of them would come up and bang on the door, despite the notice posted on the window explaining the situation. No one was happy today. Everything was spiraling out of control.

Fernando was starting to believe in a Chaco curse.

They were all gathered in the back office of the visitor center, hiding from the angry mob outside and worrying about Jim. Fernando felt powerless, unable to do anything to resolve either of their problems: the locked gates or Jim's kidnapping.

How do you search for a missing person in national park that sprawled over twenty thousand acres of high desert terrain? You would need to call out the National Guard and their helicopters in order to search an area that large. He knew from experience the deputy from the San Juan County Sheriff's Office wouldn't offer any help. He would only file a missing person report, which would get lost in all the other active missing person reports on file at the Aztec office. So what could they do with the few resources they had at their disposal?

When they moved out to the front counter their situation became even more uncomfortable.

Betty, Leroy, and Chet sat behind the counter staring at the angry faces peering at them through the windows, all of the rangers helpless to remedy the situation.

Patricia stared at Fernando, waiting for him to say or do something, but what?

When the mechanic from Cuba finally arrived, two hours later, it took him all of twenty minutes to cut both chains and open the gates. Betty, who had seniority in Jim's absence, assigned Chet to the visitor center, so as to keep him away from Marcy in the campground.

Betty would staff the campground herself so she could keep an eye on Marcy and the Bryans and hopefully prevent them from copulating in full view of the other campers.

That left Leroy to accompany Fernando and Patricia as they conducted another search for Jim, while waiting for the deputy to arrive from Aztec.

Once the gates were open it took them well over an hour to collect entry fees and admit the growing mass of unhappy visitors waiting in the parking lot. So by the time Leroy fired up the staff jeep and took off down the Chaco Loop it was approaching noon. The sun, directly overhead, scorched the road and the canyon floor. Hallucinogenic heat waves rippled across their field of vision.

"Hotter'n a motherfucker today," Leroy said as he pulled into the Pueblo Bonito parking lot. Their first job was to replace the 'Caution' tape around the fresh trenches where the looters had been digging the night before.

The new trenches were deeper and longer than on the previous mornings, as though the looters knew their window of opportunity was shrinking and were getting desperate. And reckless.

He and Patricia stood over the trenches while Leroy went back to the jeep for more tape.

"I wonder," she said quietly. "Do you think Jim could be involved in this? Could be working with the looters?"

The question took Fernando by surprise. He hadn't thought of that as a possibility, but at this point it wasn't a bad idea to consider everything. "I don't know. Never occurred to me. Should we ask Leroy what he thinks?"

She turned to look at Leroy. "No, I wouldn't ask him just yet." She offered no explanation.

Leroy quickly replaced the 'Caution' tape and then stopped to think. "I wonder if we should fill in the trenches? I mean, probably not, right? The looters will just dig it up again if they come back. And the more they dig, the more damage they do to whatever might be buried below."

Fernando considered. "It's your call. You don't want people falling in the trenches either, but I suppose the 'Caution' tape will keep them out."

So Leroy decided to leave the trenches open. The three of them began by searching Pueblo del Arroyo and Kin Kletso, walking through all the rooms and then around the perimeter of both ruins. They found no trace of Jim Murphy, except for the bicycle with the bent front tire, which they loaded onto the rack on the back of the jeep. They saw a few spots of blood on the nearby pavement, but none on the bicycle itself, no definitive indication that Murphy was attacked or injured or put up much resistance, if in fact he was kidnapped.

Leroy paused. "What now? There's no sign of him around here."

"Let's follow the wagon road and see what we find out by West Mesa," Fernando suggested. "They were headed in that direction when I saw them driving away last night."

So after unlocking the western gate they headed west on the old wagon road that he and Patricia had walked the day before, driving past the box canyon and the remnants of Highway 57. They continued on past the small ruin known as Casa Chiquita until they came to the very end of the canyon, where Chaco Wash converged with Escavada Wash to form the Chaco River. Here they stopped and climbed out of the jeep. The sun was scorching hot, splashing everything in sight with an intense white glare that reflected off the white sand that marked the confluence of the two washes.

Leroy kicked at the white sand beneath the tires. "It's difficult to drive on this sand. It's like a damned beach."

"Looks like one too," Fernando said.

Leroy laughed. "In fact, it was a beach back in the day. This is where the Chacoans had their waterworks. They built dams and canals here for irrigation and apparently even for recreation."

They looked around the confluence of the two washes for a few minutes but found no trace of Murphy and no sign that anyone had been there recently. Fernando guessed the looters had turned off the road before they reached the confluence, which meant they found a way up North Mesa, a goat trail if not an actual road. Giving up, they returned to the jeep and took turns drinking from the water bottles in the cooler Leroy had mounted on the back of the jeep.

"What now?" Leroy wanted to know.

For lack of a better idea, Fernando suggested they walk through the other ruins in the canyon, just to cover all the bases. So they drove back to the parking lot and down to Casa Rinconada and then around the loop to Hungo Pavi and Chetro Ketl. By the time they had finished searching the ruins and returned to the visitor center it was late afternoon. They were hot, tired, and out of ideas about what to do next.

At the visitor center Chet informed them that a deputy from the San Juan County Sheriff's Office had already come and gone. Just as Fernando suspected, the deputy had filed a missing person report but said the sheriff's office in Aztec did not have the manpower to search the entire canyon or the surrounding Navajo Reservation, so there wasn't much they could do to find Jim.

The deputy suggested they ask the National Park Service for additional resources and staff, so that they could conduct a comprehensive search of the park and its immediate environment. And finally, the deputy asked the same question Patricia had posed to him earlier: was there any chance Murphy might be working with the looters as an accomplice, an inside man.

"Can you believe that?" Chet asked them, clearly offended by the deputy's suggestion. "Jim is the most dedicated ranger I've ever met. He lives for this place and would never do anything to harm it."

"Still, he has to consider every possibility," Fernando said, wanting to support the sheriff, even though he knew it would not please Chet or any of the other rangers at Chaco.

When Chet went to help a customer in the gift shop, he and Patricia stepped outside and sat down at the picnic table to discuss what to do next. They decided to check in with Betty at the campground. So they traded the staff jeep for their cruiser and drove up to the campground, which was beginning to fill up as it always did May through October. Before May and after October the weather at Chaco was iffy. As hot as it was during the summer months, it was equally cold during the winter because of its altitude of six thousand feet.

They found Betty inside the ranger trailer with her clipboard, checking off the names of campers who had already arrived from her list of the night's reservations. She stepped outside of the trailer when she saw them, a hopeful look on her face. "Did you find Jim?"

"No sign of him," Fernando said, watching the hopeful look disappear from Betty's face. "We didn't come across any leads. What about you, have you had any problems here with the crowd?"

"Only Marcy and the Bryans. They were walking around stark naked this morning. I couldn't believe it. Even Paul Bryan, with his willy sticking out! It was obscene! They weren't copulating in public, but I had to go over and tell them to at least cover their bottoms. I mean, for Christ's sake, this isn't a nudist colony. Show some respect!"

He laughed. He could picture Marcy and the other two wandering around their campsite in the nude. Walking over to the restroom in the nude. Bending over their fire pit in the nude. The list went on and on.

"And Chet, I can't believe him!" Betty said. "Did you hear them last night? Chet and Marcy? Screwing all night long? Doesn't he know any better than that? With one of our campers? I'm really disappointed. I'm going to have to speak to him about Marcy tonight."

Fernando didn't know what to say about Chet and Marcy, who were consenting adults, after all. They could have been quieter, though. Betty was right about that. "Yeah," he said finally, "they made a lot of noise."

Patricia, ignoring the controversy, walked over to Betty and touched her arm. "How well do you know Jim?"

"What do you mean?"

"Just this. Jim seems to have disappeared into thin air. From what you know, is there any chance he could be working with the looters? Helping them?"

Betty looked confused. "Well...I don't know. I can't imagine him being involved with looters or whoever these people are, but I have heard him complain lately about being underpaid for all he does. I know he's applied for more lucrative positions in the National Park Service because he's ambitious and wants to advance his career. And it is true that we're underpaid, especially Jim, who's our leader and does more than anyone else here."

She shook her head, clearly troubled. " Still, I just can't believe he would betray us like that. Jim loves the park. It's like a personal thing with him, taking care of Chaco. So I don't know what to say...."

"So then you wouldn't rule it out?" Patricia asked.

"I don't know what to think. I guess not. I just don't know."

Neither did Leroy when they asked him at the visitor center, where he had gone to relieve Chet. "It's really hard to imagine," he responded. "Jim's straight as an arrow. Maybe too officious for his own good, because everyone here lets him make all the decisions and do all the work. I'm sorry, I just don't see Jim getting involved with a bunch of looters."

Patricia suggested they search Jim's unit, so the two of them spent a half hour going through the ranger's belongings, starting with his desk and kitchen cabinets. Then they searched his closets and the drawers of his bedside bureau for anything that might indicate he was implicated in the illegal digging. They found nothing, except a receipt from an Indian arts gallery in Gallup for one item, a large 'Anasazi' pot, placed on consignment this past April. He pocketed the receipt in case he wanted to follow up on this later.

They were just finishing and were about to leave when Chet burst through the door. "Quick, come to the visitor center!" Chet said, brushing his blond hair out of is eyes. "We need you to take a look at what just came in."

They followed Chet back to the visitor center, which was empty at this late hour, except for Leroy sitting at the computer behind the front desk. He waved for them to come around the counter.

"Take a look at this," Leroy said. "It just came in as a 'Contact Us" comment on our website."

Fernando and Patricia looked over at the screen and read: "Your friend is bound and gagged and exposed to the elements in one of the ruins on top of the mesa. If you want to see him alive, then keep out of the canyon tonight and tomorrow night. If you don't, your friend is a dead man."

"Now what?" Leroy asked.

The question lingered in the silence of the room.

13

After closing for the night they met in the visitor center to debate how to respond to the extortion threat. Leroy and Chet thought the warning was likely a ruse, arguing they should continue searching for Jim during the day and patrolling the canyon at night. Furthermore, they argued Jim would want them to do precisely that–keep after the looters. Patricia and Betty disagreed. They countered that, given the unknowns, caution would be a better option. So they reached a compromise: they would look for Jim during the day but stay out of the canyon at night, which is what the kidnappers wanted.

Chet wasn't happy about the decision. "Okay, if that's what you want, but if Jim really is being held in one of the mesa ruins, how do we know which one?" he asked. "Where do we start?"

"Well, it seems logical to start with the Peñasco Blanco ruin on West Mesa, because that's where Fernando saw them heading the night Jim disappeared," Patricia said.

Everyone eventually agreed and adjourned for the night, hoping to get a better sleep than the night before when Marcy slept over with Chet and raised the roof with her screaming.

The next morning, after the park opened, Fernando and Patricia met Leroy in the parking lot. Leroy filled a cooler with bottles of water and then loaded it on the back of the staff jeep. He also brought a supply of apples, oranges, and granola bars in case any of them required quick energy.

Then the three of them drove off to search Peñasco Blanco, following the old wagon road west beyond the Kin Kletso ruin. He had no idea how far or how hard the hike would be, but he soon found out. Leroy drove to the edge of West Mesa, just before the convergence of the Chaco and Escavada washes where they had been the day before. He parked in the shade along the cliff.

Leroy hoisted his backpack. "It's only about a mile or so from here...well, maybe two."

Fernando felt reassured. Surely, he could manage a couple of miles, even though his legs were stiff from last night.

They followed the trail down into the shallow but wide Chaco Wash. Walking through the willow and saltbush and then over the sandy bottom of the arroyo seemed easy enough. He noticed all the animal tracks in the sand, coyotes and deer or elk mostly, since there were no dogs at Chaco. No one brought their pets here because they weren't allowed near the ruins and also because it was too damned hot for dogs during the summer months. The more time he spent here, the more he began to wonder if Chaco wasn't too damned hot for people too.

So far, so good, but soon after crossing the arroyo the trail began a steep climb up the rocky mesa. The trail might be only a mile or two in distance, but it involved a climb of several hundred feet up the cliff, zig-zagging from one switchback to another, Fernando soon realized. Not an easy slog for a man with legs still stiff from a midnight bike ride from hell.

When his knees started barking, Fernando asked Leroy to slow down so he could keep up with them. Leroy didn't seem to mind. In fact, he enjoyed acting as a self-appointed tour guide, pointing out certain trailside attractions along the way. Leroy stopped for several minutes at a pictograph that was supposedly a representation of the 1054 supernova, which was visible in the daytime over Chaco for twenty-three days and in the nighttime sky for over two years.

The Chacoans were ancient astronomers, Leroy said, aligning their Great Houses to solar and lunar cycles and recording important cosmic events in their cliff art. He went on to discuss Chaco's elite rulers and how their knowledge of astronomy gave them the authority to rule. That is, their knowledge and self-proclaimed control of cosmic events gave them the authority to rule.

Fernando enjoyed the lecture while it lasted, but when they started up the trail again his legs began to cramp badly. From the pictograph on he was running on fumes, so that when they finally crested the top of West Mesa, he was ready for a break. Leroy and Patricia were far ahead, already searching the ruin for any sign of Jim. By the time he reached the broken outer walls of the Peñasco Blanco ruin they had already determined the site was clean and were heading back down the trail.

Fernando stopped, short of breath. With his hands on his hips, he watched the two of them walk right past him and begin the descent, leaving him winded and tired and generally pissed. To hell with them, he decided, sitting down on a nearby ridge of rock and relaxing, He knew from years of experience that going down would be harder on the knees than coming up, so what was the hurry?

Soon he heard Patricia shouting, "Fernando? Where are you?"

"I'm up here!" he shouted right back. "Where you left me!"

Now maybe they understood, because they waited patiently while he climbed down, trying to take small gentle steps that were easy on his knees.

"Sorry, Fernando, didn't mean to leave you up there," Patricia said.

Leroy laughed. "That's all we would need, another member of the team missing!"

Fernando failed to see the humor, but he was relieved to find that when they started down again, the three of them moved at his pace. It was past noon when they made it back to the jeep. They had nothing to show for their morning's work. Jim could have been on another planet for all they knew.

They drove back to the visitor center to check in with Chet. No news, Chet said, except that Betty had called and wanted to speak with Fernando as soon as possible. So Fernando left Patricia at the visitor center and drove the cruiser up to the campground to meet Betty. He found her sitting at a picnic table outside the ranger station eating lunch in the shade of an umbrella. She waved as he drove up and parked next to the station and climbed out of the cruiser.

"Have a seat and share some lunch with me," she said. She offered him half of her chicken salad sandwich and placed a bowl of fruit between them.

He sat down, relieved to have an opportunity to rest.

"There's a cold drink in the cooler here." She reached in and pulled out a bottle of water and handed it to him. "There. You look hungry. And hot!"

"Yeah, it's exhausting trying to keep up with these young people. Thanks."

"Did you get my message?"

"I did. What's up?"

"Well, this may or may not be something of interest, but I thought you should know. This afternoon we had a visitor by the name of Earl Skinner. At least that's the name he gave me. A little guy, but quite muscular. Said he was working on an oil rig out on Highway

Five Fifty and wanted to check out the campground in case he wanted to get away for a night or two and do some hiking.

"Anyway, he got involved with Marcy one way or another, you can imagine, and the two of them were going at it like dogs in heat. Afterwards she made a point of coming up here and telling me that she was a sex therapist, not to worry about her trysts. Imagine that. She said she helped men with sexual problems, and women too. Personally, I think she's just a hooker, but who knows?"

Fernando laughed. "Probably a good guess."

"The thing is, this Earl guy came up to me on his way out of the campground and asked if we had discovered any illegal digging in the canyon recently. Right out of the blue."

"What did you tell him?"

"Well, for starters, I said we were always worried about people digging in the canyon, which is illegal. Then—and get this—he asked if we patrol the park at night, pretending to be concerned about whether we were doing enough to keep the looters out. I can't remember his exact words, but he made some comment about the full moon being an opportune time for looters and asked if we were going to patrol tonight. That sounded suspicious to me, so I shut up then. I didn't say one way or the other. In fact, I didn't say another word."

He was interested now. "Really? So you think this guy might be one of the looters?"

"I don't know, but why would he come over to ask me if we were patrolling tonight? You see what I mean."

"What was he driving?"

"A red pickup, Ford I think. Looked fairly new. I didn't get the license plate number."

"I think I better go talk to Marcy," Fernando said.

So after finishing his sandwich he thanked Betty and walked over to the tent circle, where Marcy and the Bryans were sharing Marcy's tent.

He had been trying to avoid Marcy and the Bryans, who he'd not met, but apparently that was not going to be possible. He would see for himself if they were as bad as their reputation.

He saw Marcy's tent up ahead, a large blue and white contraption with a nylon extension over the doorway. It looked to be at least a five-person tent, maybe larger. She had strung a makeshift clothesline between two bushes beside the tent, where skimpy shorts, halter-tops, and women's undergarments flapped obscenely in the wind. She had the usual camping gear outside on her picnic table and a stack of firewood next to the fire pit.

Then he noticed Marcy. She sat in a fold-back camping chair wearing a bikini bottom and no top, watching him approach with keen interest. She looked even skinnier than she had the other night, with a wisp of blond hair dangling across her forehead, her bare breasts tanning in the sun.

"Hi, honey, I wondered when you were going to come over. I saw you looking at me the other day. I can read minds, you know. It's one of my many powers, along with sexual restoration."

"Restoration?"

"That's right," she said. "If it's broken, I'll fix it. And I don't need no damned Viagra!"

Fernando laughed. If only Estelle could hear Marcy. She wouldn't talk to him for a week! He showed Marcy his badge. "Detective Fernando Lopez, Santa Fe Police Department."

"Santa Fe? You're a long way from home, honey. You must be lonely. Even police detectives need therapy sometimes, you know."

"I'm good. I need to ask you some questions about Earl Skinner, the guy who was here earlier. Remember him?"

"Earl? Yeah, baby! He was hot!"

"So I hear. Did he say what he was doing here?"

"Just relaxing. I helped him out with that," she said, laughing. "But he told me his name was Simmons, Earl Simmons."

"Did he mention digging in the ruins?"

"Not to me he didn't."

"Did he say where he was working? Give you a name, a company?"

"He said he was working on an oil rig over by Nageezi. Fracking. I don't recollect the name."

He considered. "By the way, where are the Bryans?"

"They just left to go back to their RV," she said. "We finished our afternoon nuptials, taking turns, you know. We like to mix it up freestyle when we're not practicing our rituals."

"Rituals?" Fernando made the mistake of asking.

"Sure. Sex is all about spirituality and its rituals. You'd understand that if you worked with an experienced therapist like me."

Marcy leaned forward, looking deeply into his eyes. "I can initiate you into the world of spiritual sex, the rituals and ceremonies of fulfillment that you never knew existed."

When he looked dubious, Marcy added. "I'm a licensed therapist."

"So I hear. "

"Never had any complaints," she said.

Fernando laughed, starting to get uncomfortable.

"Well, if you remember any more details about this Earl character, please let me know. You can reach me at the visitor center or the staff barracks. Just ask Betty to get in touch with me, okay?"

"Will do. Don't be a stranger, now."

Leaving the tent circle, Fernando decided to stop by the Bryans' RV at campsite 18. He spotted the sleek Mercedes Sprinter from across the campground. Leroy had been right about the RV, it was a piece of art. He had never been inside one, but he told himself that if and when he retired, and if he could convince Estelle, he would buy one of these Sprinters and they could spend a good part of the winter on the road in southern Arizona or maybe southern California. Not everyone knew it, but Santa Fe could get damned cold in the winter.

The Bryans waved as he walked over to their campsite. Or at least Paul waved. June, a mousy little thing with close-cropped blue hair, was meditating in leotards on a yoga pad near the cliff. She flashed him a smile and then turned away.

"Greetings," Paul said, an equally thin, middle-aged man wearing skimpy swimming trunks and flip-flops. His dark hair was so heavily moussed it looked like gelatin.

"Detective Fernando Lopez, Santa Fe Police," he said, shaking Paul's hand firmly.

"Glad to meet you, detective. We're Santa Feans, too. We moved here from Sedona three years ago and love Santa Fe. You might have seen our shop on Canyon Road, Essentia?"

"The sex shop?"

"Oh, well, we're more than a sex shop," Paul said, not at all offended by his question. "Yes, we sell a variety of sexual enhancements, but we also offer a number of other New Age services. June over there is a karmic wound and energy healer," he said, pointing to June, who was still meditating on her yoga pad near the cliff.

June ignored them.

"So if you need a little help healing a karmic wound or adjusting your energy field, June can work wonders for you. Just between you and me, karmic healers like June are much more effective than psychiatrists with all their dark Freudian nonsense and their stupefying drugs."

Paul pointed toward Marcy's tent on the other side of the

campground. "And Marcy, our colleague, is a wonderful sex therapist. Sexuality is ninety percent spiritual, you know, and only a mere ten percent physical. We offer hands-on therapy, not just personal counseling or pharmaceuticals. That is, we actually come into people's homes to perform with our patients. We bring a variety of toys and apparatuses, as well as therapeutic oils that stimulate performance such as eucalyptus and especially ylang ylang."

Fernando had no idea what the hell Paul was talking about. Ylang ylang?

"That's how we met Marcy, during a threesome. We teach the circle orgasm technique, where we all hold hands and I ejaculate into one of the women, which sends shockwaves through the hands of all the others until everyone orgasms at once. We can show you, if you like."

"No thanks."

"You're never too old, if that's your worry," Paul said. "Marcy is a wonder at reviving the libido."

Fernando smiled. "So I hear."

"We also specialize in aura photography," Paul continued, not missing a beat with his sales pitch. "We have the only AuraCam six thousand in Santa Fe—that's a specialized camera that captures the electromagnetic field surrounding the body, which we call the aura. You have to go all the way to Sedona to find another AuraCam six thousand. I can tell, just by looking at you from an angle, that you have a lot of red in your aura. Maybe a little green too, but red is definitely dominant."

Paul held up his hands, framing him as if he were looking through a camera. "It's not surprising you would have a lot of red, given your profession. It makes sense that your aura would suggest power and passion—"

Ignoring the sales pitch Fernando asked, "I hear you also collect old rugs and pots, is that right?"

Taken aback, Paul stopped in mid-sentence. "No, not really. Who told you that, if I may ask?"

"You told Leroy Roybal, one of the park rangers here."

"Well, we have a few old Navajo rugs and things, but it's not part of our work at Essentia. It's separate."

"It's a private collection, then."

Paul nodded. "Sort of."

"Thanks," he said. "If I have any more questions, I know where to find you. Maybe I'll stop by Essentia one of these days and get my aura photographed. Just to make sure I have an aura."

Paul laughed. "Please do. It's on the house."

He smiled, making a mental note to check out the Bryans' private collection as soon as he returned to Santa Fe.

Paul waved as he walked away.

Over by the cliff June smiled, sitting with one leg cocked behind her head in a position that made his entire body ache just looking at her.

14

Back at the visitor center, Patricia and Leroy already had plans to hike to the top of South Mesa to search the Tsin Kletsin ruin, the Great House protecting the southern entrance to the canyon. They had chosen to search South Mesa next, over North Mesa, because that's where the interloper with the torch had gone on the night of the fire in Casa Rinconada. Fernando had his fill of South Mesa that night, but the two of them were wired and ready to go, with backpacks and water bottles and sun hats.

Chet, bored with counter duty, begged Leroy to change places with him, but Leroy declined, happy to be outside hiking. Like Jim, he seemed to have unlimited energy. Fernando understood why they would make good park rangers.

Leroy turned to him with a warning. "The South Mesa trail is difficult. It's a six- mile hike round trip with steep inclines most of the way. You need to be in good shape to do this one."

"Are you trying to tell me something, Leroy?" Fernando asked, half joking. He hadn't missed the implication that he was not fit enough to accompany them. He supposed it was a reasonable assumption given his performance going up West Mesa.

Leroy tried to apologize, but Fernando waved him off since he was thinking the same thing. In fact, he had planned to send the two of them up South Mesa while he looked for Earl's pickup out on Highway 550 near Nageezi, where all the oil rigs and frackers were located. He wanted to know more about Earl Skinner, AKA Earl Simmons. Why would Earl ask about illegal digging and night patrols unless he was involved with the looters? He intended to find out.

Patricia and Leroy left first, driving off in the staff jeep with all their supplies. After they were gone, Chet saw his opportunity and approached him.

"Listen, I have an idea. Why don't we call Betty and have her come over here. She could staff the visitor center while Marcy holds down the fort over at the campground. That way I could come with you as backup. It could be dangerous out there by yourself, for sure."

He looked at Chet skeptically. "Marcy? You want to put Marcy in charge of the campground?"

"Yeah, she'd be fine. Really. She's a lot more capable than you think. She's a therapist, you know."

"So I keep hearing," Fernando said. "Call Betty and see what she says. It's your decision, not mine."

So Chet called Betty and asked if she would take over at the visitor center and turn the campground over to Marcy. Not a good move. Fernando could hear Betty yelling in the phone, giving Chet a piece of her mind about his irresponsibility and Marcy's idiocy. Then she started in on his sexual antics with Marcy and his inconsiderate behavior in keeping them awake all night long. He kept trying to put down the phone but Betty continued her tirade, assaulting him with a long list of grievances, some predating their current troubles.

"Okay, okay, chill out!" Chet said, hanging up on her finally. Then he turned to Fernando. "What's her problem?"

"Marcy, I would imagine."

With that, Fernando left a brooding Chet to his duties at the visitor center.

The day was looking up now that he didn't have to hike to the top of another damned mesa. He took the cruiser and drove the sixteen long miles to Highway 550, stopping first for gas at the Nageezi station. Driving around the Chaco Loop was burning up a lot of gasoline.

After fueling the cruiser, he went inside to buy a bottle of water and to ask the attendant, a young Navajo woman with a friendly smile and a nose ring, if she knew anyone by the name of Earl who drove a red Ford pickup and worked at one of the nearby rigs.

She shook her head. "No, I don't really talk to them. They're not all that friendly, not to me anyway."

"You mean the people who work on the oil rigs?"

She looked at him carefully for a long moment and then added. "And Anglos in general."

He thanked her and took his drink outside. From the gas station, situated on the top of a high knoll, he could look east toward Cuba and the Jemez Mountains. Oil rigs dotted the entire landscape as far as the eye could see. Black, greasy pumps humped the land, leaving spills and pools of crude oil everywhere. Huge trucks drove in and out of makeshift roads that crisscrossed the high desert terrain. Further up he saw the trailers and fracking units with their cranes and water tanks injecting pressurized water into the ground, cracking the earth wide open.

It was a view of spoliation, nothing more, nothing less.

The supporters of fracking argued that it was a quick way to find oil and that it provided jobs, as if there weren't other forms of energy that would provide jobs, especially in a place like New Mexico with its ample solar and wind energy. The opponents argued that fracking was destroying the environment and causing earthquakes, which is why the Sierra Club and other environmental groups had been protesting and filing lawsuits against fracking, especially in fragile areas like Nageezi where 1,200-year-old ruins were endangered. After all, Chaco Canyon was a UNESCO World Heritage site, one of a kind.

Personally he had nothing but contempt for the frackers and the oil industry in general. The country had been drunk on oil for far too long, willfully participating in the destruction of the planet. It was time to move on while the planet was still habitable, if it still was. He had his doubts. That was his view and he didn't plan to change it any time soon, no matter what propaganda the greedy bastards who controlled the oil industry put out to control the befuddled masses. Befuddled, he liked that word. It explained a whole lot.

After he finished grumbling to himself, he put away his bottle of water and drove east on Highway 550 looking for red pickup trucks at the oil rigs along the highway. Problem was, he saw half a dozen red pickups before he'd barely gone one mile. Finally, just to give it a shot, he turned onto a gravel road leading to a site where a red pickup was parked over by a trailer. When he stepped out of the cruiser, he could smell the oil saturating the ground, stinking up the place. He wondered what would happen if someone dropped a lit match. Would the whole damned place go up in a cloud of fire and smoke?

He walked over to the trailer, nestled at the base of a ridge of black basalt cones streaked with gray that looked like the spine of some great beast partially buried in the earth. Old volcanoes had created this landscape, and if the frackers had their way earthquakes might recreate it and in doing so destroy the ancestral homeland of every group of Native Americans in the Four Corners area. It was a scientifically proven fact that fracking caused earthquakes. Just look at what was happening in Oklahoma, where fracking had already caused thousands of small earthquakes, even though the frackers and their supporters refused to acknowledge the facts.

Bamboozlers, all of them.

The door to the trailer was open, so he stepped inside.

"Can I help you?" a tall man wearing a baseball cap asked. He stood overlooking a large topographic map spread out on his desk.

Fernando showed his badge. "I'm looking for a guy named Earl Simmons, maybe Skinner. He drives a red Ford pickup. Does anyone like that work here?"

The man shook his head. "No, nobody by that name works here. Never has, as far as I know. You might try some of the other rigs. They're all up and down this highway."

"So I've noticed."

"I'm sorry, but you'll have to vacate the property. We don't allow nonemployees on the grounds."

Fernando gave a mock salute and walked back to the cruiser. He tried one more rig but received the same response: no Earl, never heard of an Earl, now get off the property.

Giving up, he decided to head back to Chaco and take it easy for a while, before Leroy and Patricia enlisted him to climb up another mesa to look for Jim. When he drove into the canyon he stopped first at the campground to check with Betty, who had nothing new to report, and then continued on down to the staff barracks, which was rapidly becoming a ghost town with Pete Chavez dead and Jim Murphy missing and possibly dead. Who was next?

Fernando decided to take a short nap on the beat-up sofa before thinking about dinner. He no more than lay down on the dirty corduroy cushions before he was sound asleep, dreaming of a picnic he and Estelle and their two daughters had enjoyed one summer day many years ago at Canjilon Lakes. Pleasant memories of the girls when they were young, picking flowers on the banks of the lake and playing hide-and-seek among the ponderosa pines. The surface of the lake looked like glass, reflecting the deep blue sky and the bright sunshine shimmering on the water....

Wet, warm lips brought him to the surface of consciousness. He reached out to put his arms around Estelle, but when he opened his eyes he saw the big gray eyes and open mouth of Marcy sticking her wet tongue in and out of his mouth. Wearing only a tiny bikini, she climbed on top of him and caressed his body all over with her roving hands.

"What? Get off me! What are you doing?"

"I saw the way you were looking at me earlier, baby. Marcy's here now, I'll take care of you," she moaned, reaching between his legs while rubbing her crotch against his hip bone.

"Are you crazy? I'm a married man. Happily married!" He pushed her away from him roughly.

"Owww," she said, plopping down on the wooden floor. "Oh, baby, why didn't you tell me you like rough sex? Have I got the toys for you!"

"No! I don't want to have sex with you. Get out!"

"No sex with Marcy? No therapy?" She put her hands on her hips and glared at him, as if she couldn't believe he would really turn her down, that *any* man would turn her down.

"No therapy!" Fernando repeated.

"Well, detective, I guess I was wrong about you," she pouted. "Your loss, baby. Marcy had something special in mind for you."

With that, she picked herself up and dusted off her bikini, the first time he had seen her fully dressed, if wearing a bikini counted as fully dressed.

Marcy turned her back and headed for the door. She turned around before leaving and gave him the finger. Then she slammed the door shut behind her, ending their therapy session.

15

Fernando lay awake most of the night. He kept imagining a mob of looters digging in Pueblo Bonito, smashing bones and ancient artifacts, piling up mounds of earth and human skulls until they found what they were looking for: Wetherill's hidden artifacts. He tossed and turned on the narrow sofa, agonizing over their decision not to go after the looters until Jim was either found or released. Then he worried that he had given up too soon trying to find Earl when he was in Nageezi among the oil rigs and frackers. The night was one nightmare after another.

When the first light of morning came splashing through the curtains, he was already up and pacing around the tiny unit. He'd had a change of heart. No more delays. They had to go after the looters tonight. He and Patricia and maybe Leroy would be waiting for them at Bonito if and when they made an appearance. That meant they would have to find Jim today, before nightfall, if he was indeed being held captive in one of the ruins on North Mesa, which was the only mesa they hadn't yet searched.

If Jim was working with the looters, well, that was a possibility he didn't want to consider at the moment. That would definitely complicate matters. In ways he didn't even want to think about.

Once again, they all gathered at the visitor center before opening the park. They agreed on the same division of labor. Betty would monitor the campground, Chet would staff the visitor center, and Leroy would accompany him and Patricia on a search of North Mesa. Leroy warned them that to get to the top of North Mesa they would have to climb a steep ancient stairway in the cliff behind Kin Kletso. He said they would need lots of water for the hike, which could be as long as three or four miles over rough terrain. He would carry the water they would need in his backpack; he and Patricia would just have to worry about getting themselves up the mesa and down the trail to Pueblo Alto.

Leroy turned to Fernando and Patricia. "What do you think? Are you two up to the climb?"

"I'm ready," Fernando said, hiding his irritation.

Patricia ignored Leroy.

Even though he hadn't slept, Fernando felt energized today. His legs were still a little stiff, but not enough to slow him down. More than anything else he just wanted this investigation to come to a conclusion. He sensed a finality to this day, which gave him the lift, the adrenaline rush he needed to make it through the day come what may. Plus he wanted to show Leroy a thing or two. He resented having his physical ability questioned.

As before, they loaded the Igloo cooler on the back of the jeep and drove off together. Leroy stopped to open the gate and then drove them to the Pueblo del Arroyo parking lot, where they pulled in next to the covered picnic tables. Leroy hoisted up his heavy backpack, supplied with three liters of water, and led them down the trail toward Kin Kletso.

While they loaded up for the hike, several cars pulled into the parking lot and an assortment of hikers took off, some to Kin Kletso and others heading for Peñasco Blanco on the West Mesa Trail.

They followed a group of four hikers around behind Kin Kletso to the ancient stairway, which didn't look like much of a damned stairway to him. The people ahead of them were climbing on a series of boulders until, halfway to the top, the cliff split into a three-foot wide crevice inside of which he saw steps carved out of the sandstone a millennia ago. Climbing over the boulders would be the hardest part. If he could get past the boulders, he could make it to the top of the mesa.

Leroy led the way, with Patricia second and him bringing up the rear. Nearing the top, one of the people ahead slipped and fell back into Leroy. For a moment he thought they would all go down like a row of dominoes, plunging back into the canyon. But Leroy was experienced at climbing these ancient stairways and caught himself by grabbing hold of a ledge on one side of the crevice. Then he paused long enough for the people ahead to reach the top of the mesa, so as not to repeat the chain reaction if one of them fell back again.

Once on top they walked out into the sunshine, looking out on a vast panorama of mesas and distant mountain ranges surrounding the canyon. Leroy didn't waste any time sightseeing. Instead, he led them straight ahead on the trail that ran east along the edge of the cliff to a roped-off area designated by a wooden sign as the Pueblo Bonito Overlook. From the overlook they looked down on the enormity of the Great House, a geometrical maze of circular kivas and rectangular rooms.

The four people ahead of them stopped to take photos with their cell phones, but Leroy pressed on, with Fernando and Patricia following close behind. The trail turned due north and climbed a small ridge to what remained of the Great North Road that at one time had connected Chaco with its northern outliers at Salmon and Aztec ruins. When they crested yet another ridge of rock they caught a glimpse of the Pueblo Alto ruin on a hill far ahead of them. The distant ruin grew larger as they made their way up the long, sloping hillside.

Leroy stopped for a water break before they started up the last stretch to Pueblo Alto. Not even noon and already the morning had turned blazing hot, with not a shade tree in sight anywhere on the mesa.

Fernando was sweating profusely under his sunhat and around his neck. He took a handkerchief out of his pocket and wiped the sweat from his face. When Patricia handed him the water bottle, he drank his fill and then handed it back to Leroy.

Leroy turned to them. "You ready?"

Neither Fernando nor Patricia responded.

Just as Leroy put the water bottle back in his backpack they heard shouting coming from up on the hill. Someone was shouting at them. Soon they saw two people wearing shorts and T-shirts come running down the trail from Pueblo Alto shouting and waving at them, trying to get their attention. The two of them appeared frightened, even hysterical.

"Help! We need help!" the first one shouted, a young man who looked to be in his early twenties. His companion, a young woman of about the same age, followed a few yards behind him.

They waited for the two runners to approach, uncertain and a bit wary of the situation. He stepped to the side of the trail and tried to guess which one needed help, the young man or the young woman. Had one of them been bitten by a rattlesnake, a not uncommon occurrence in the desert Southwest? Or had one of them, or perhaps someone else, taken a fall or had an accident farther up the trail? Neither of them showed any signs of injury as far as he could tell by the way they were running quickly down the trail.

The young man arrived out of breath.

"There's a dying man up there," he panted, hands on his knees, trying to get his breath. "He's dying, or maybe he's dead already, I don't know. His face is covered with blood and his hands and feet are taped together. He doesn't seem to be breathing. We need to get help fast. He's dying!"

"No...I think he's one of the walking dead," the young woman corrected her companion, once she was able to catch her breath. She wore a UNM baseball cap pulled down over her brown ponytail. "You've seen them in movies and on TV. This one's face is all black and decomposing, with blood all over and rotting flesh that stinks the closer you get to him! He's really gross."

Fernando raised his hand to put a stop to the hysteria. "So is he dead, or is he dying, or what?"

"He's in-between," the woman said. "You know, that liminal state between living and dying."

Actually, Fernando didn't know. You're either dead or you're alive, he wanted to say but didn't.

"Where is he? At Pueblo Alto?" Patricia asked.

"No, no...he's in that small ruin north of Alto."

"Rabbit Run," Leroy said. "It's about a hundred yards north of Alto. Strictly off limits to hikers, but some people go up there anyway. It's hard to keep them out without more staffing."

"Show us," Fernando said.

"Not me, I won't go back there and take a chance of being infected," the young woman said to her companion. "Don't go. You're crazy if you go back there! You'll become one of them!"

"What chance? What's she talking about?" Patricia asked.

Neither he nor Leroy responded.

"Follow me, I'll show you," the young man said, ignoring his companion's advice.

"Then I'll meet you at the car," the young woman said. She turned and hurried down the trail toward the parking lot without looking back at her companion. Not a glance.

So they followed the young man up the hill to the Pueblo Alto ruin, a mid-sized Great House with collapsed walls and kivas that seemed to sink into the center of the one-story ruin as if the ruin were built around a sinkhole. Two middle-aged women meandered around the perimeter on the far side of the ruin. Otherwise, Pueblo Alto looked deserted.

When they crested the hill on which Pueblo Alto was built

Fernando could see the small Rabbit Run ruin farther down the trail on the left. From this distance it was hardly more than a pile of stones. And he saw something else, what looked like an animal of some sort thrashing about in the dirt. When the figure rose to its knees and tried to stand up, he realized it was human. He watched as the person collapsed and again struggled to its knees.

"There! That's him!" the young man said, pointing.

"Wait--I think that's Jim!" Leroy said.

Leroy ran on ahead to help the injured person, convinced it was Jim and not one of the walking dead, while he and Patricia followed behind with the young man.

As they approached Rabbit Run, they saw the injured man was indeed Jim. Leroy sat down next to his injured friend and cradled him in his lap as he would an infant.

Fernando understood why when he came close enough to see Murphy's swollen face, with one black eye and a broken nose. His thin blond hair was caked with dirt and blood, as were his clothes. Strands of broken duct tape dangled from his wrists and legs. Jim must have freed himself somehow and called for help, frightening the two young people who happened to be hiking near the ruin.

"Christ, give him some water," Fernando said, but Patricia was already on the ground holding a water bottle while Jim gulped down huge mouthfuls of water nonstop until she pulled the bottle away, telling him to drink slowly. When she pulled back he fought her for the bottle, making a low groaning sound that sounded more like a wounded animal than a human.

"Take it easy, my friend, we're here now. We're gonna get you to a hospital. Just hold on, okay."

"Here, let's try to move him out of the sun, maybe back against the rear wall," Fernando said, realizing Jim's face was badly sunburned as well as beaten to a pulp. So he and Leroy each took an arm and moved him carefully into the shade behind the rear wall, the only wall still standing at Rabbit Run. Even so, Jim cried out in pain and tried to fight them off when they went to lift him. He moaned and gurgled as if trying to communicate something to his rescuers, but they couldn't understand anything he said.

Now that his friend was out of the sun, Leroy quickly called the visitor center and told Chet they'd found Jim on North Mesa and told him to call the University of New Mexico Hospital, the only level one trauma center in the state, and ask for a medevac helicopter to lift Murphy out of the canyon. He gave Morris their location near Rabbit Run and their GPS coordinates.

"And make it fast, Chet. He's in bad shape, I don't know how long he can hold on. There's no other way to get him down off the mesa."

Chet called back a few minutes later to say the helicopter would be there in about forty minutes.

Taking advantage of the lull in activity, the young man who had been the first to find Jim said, "I guess I'll leave now that you guys are taking care of him. Okay with you?"

"Before you go, let me get your name and telephone number, just in case we need to reach you," Fernando said. "How did you find him, by the way?"

"We heard what sounded like growling as we walked down the trail to Rabbit Run. Then we saw him stumble out of the ruin and fall down. I thought he was dying. We panicked and started running and yelling for help. That's when we saw the three of you."

The young man wrote his name and number on a piece of paper and handed it to Fernando. "Good luck!"

They thanked him as he hurried off to catch up with his girlfriend.

While they waited, Fernando tried to talk with Jim, who was sitting up now leaning against rear the wall of the ruin. "Jim—are you awake? Can you tell us what happened?"

Jim made the same low groaning sound as before. He rolled his head from side to side, trying to focus first on Leroy and then on Fernando. Suddenly his eyes rolled back in his head.

"Who did this to you, Jim? Can you tell us what happened?"

Jim reeled from side to side, mustering all his energy in an attempt to speak. "No...don' know...no can...iff't wuz...wha' happ'n... wether'll gosh...kill me...nah'sur...tak'n me...here."

"What? What's he saying?" Fernando asked the others.

"He said Wetherill's ghost tried to kill him," Patricia said.

Fernando and Leroy looked at one another.

Finally Fernando said, "He's not in his right mind."

"Maybe," Patricia said.

Jim's eyes rolled back in his head again and he seemed to lose consciousness altogether.

Leroy panicked and tried to shake Murphy awake. "Stay with us, Jim! Come on, buddy, wake up!"

"Don't!" Patricia said, kneeling and reaching for Murphy's wrist. "He has a pulse and he's still breathing. He's just exhausted. He should be fine once we get him to the hospital."

So they waited impatiently for the medevac to arrive, Leroy pacing back and forth along the rear wall, worrying that it would be too late to save his friend, just as they had been unable to save Pete Chavez earlier. Fernando sat in the shade of the wall next to Jim fanning himself and the injured ranger with his notebook. By now it was hotter than a motherfucker, as Leroy had said. Patricia sat quietly by herself on a sheet of rock off to the side, watching the others and the sky.

Nearly an hour later they heard the chopper approaching before they actually saw it in the sky. When they did, Fernando walked out onto the open mesa waving his arms overhead until the pilot spotted him and dipped his blades to acknowledge contact. It took two fly-bys for the pilot to find a reasonably flat place to land about fifty yards northwest of Rabbit Run, at which point the pilot eased the chopper down, its blades kicking up a dust storm of sand, tumbleweed, and dead cheat grass. The chopper tipped slightly when it set down, and then steadied itself on the soft sandy terrain.

As soon as the pilot cut the engine, two medics jumped out and ran over to where they huddled against the wall of Rabbit Run. The medics were both young men wearing blue jackets and were incredibly efficient. One checked Murphy's vitals, while the other gathered the essential information they needed from the three of them. They carefully placed Murphy on a stretcher and carried him directly to the chopper, where they immediately started an IV to rehydrate the injured man.

Murphy, still unconscious, was totally oblivious to what was going on around him.

'Which one of you wants to come with us?" the older of the medics asked. "We'll need one of you to do the paperwork."

Fernando and Patricia looked at Leroy.

"I'll go with you," Leroy said. "We work together. We're friends."

"Okay, let's go!" the medic said.

"Wait. How will I get back here?" Leroy asked.

"I'll call my office in Albuquerque," Patricia said. "Someone will drive you back, probably tomorrow. You'll have to spend the night."

"Okay, just tell Betty what's happened. She's the next in command."

Leroy climbed aboard. The pilot engaged the chopper, its blades once again chewing up the ground cover north of Rabbit Run. Then it rose slowly above the canyon rim, swerved, and headed southeast toward Albuquerque.

Fernando and Patricia watched the chopper until it disappeared into the horizon. Suddenly they found themselves surrounded by a deafening silence. No chopper, no voices, no sounds of any kind.

"Well, I guess we can eliminate Jim as a suspect," Fernando said finally.

"Looks that way."

"Without Leroy, it's just the two of us now," he said.

"Doesn't matter. Tonight's the night. We get them tonight. No more delays," she said flatly. With that, she turned and began the long walk down the trail to the canyon floor.

16

Two hours later, when they finally made it back to the visitor center, they were surprised to find the parking lot empty and the center closed, with a piece of paper reading "Visitors should report to the campground for entry fees and passes" taped to the front door. Since when does a national park visitor center close during the day in the middle of the summer tourist season? Fernando wondered.

Patricia was thinking the same thing.

"I don't like the look of this," she said. "Something's wrong here."

Exchanging the jeep for their cruiser, they drove quickly to the campground, where a long line of cars had formed, waiting to get a permit to enter the park from the attendant. They found Chet frantically trying to deal with the arriving tourists one vehicle at a time, while Betty attended to Marcy, who sat hunched over the picnic table weeping. Marcy wore a stylish silk robe that actually covered her body, a first since she'd arrived at the park. They saw why she cried as soon as they pulled off the road and jumped out of the cruiser. Marcy's face was red and swollen and a thin trickle of blood dripped from her nose. She wept even harder when she saw them approaching, the sight of Fernando adding insult to injury.

Betty motioned for Patricia to take Marcy back to her tent. "Please," she whispered.

"Come with me, let's get you cleaned up," Patricia said, putting her arm around Marcy and directing her away from the ranger station.

Marcy walked off with her head resting on Patricia's shoulder.

"What happened?" Fernando asked.

Betty shrugged. "Some guy beat her up this morning. I had to call Chet to come over because she was hysterical. I was going to take her to the Urgent Care in Aztec, but now she's refusing."

Just then the Bryans' Mercedes RV came rumbling down the

campground road much too fast, spewing gravel and rock to either side of the big vehicle. Paul sat hunched over the steering wheel and June sat frozen in the passenger's seat. Both stared straight ahead, ignoring Chet and Betty standing in front of the line of vehicles waiting to enter the campground. Chet and Betty scurried out of the way as the RV roared by them. The Bryans were obviously in a big hurry to leave.

Fernando managed to catch up with Patricia and Marcy as they walked along the road to the tent circle. He noticed Marcy had a noticeable limp. When they arrived at Marcy's tent, Patricia turned to him and gave him the sign to back off. She went inside the tent with Marcy, while he waited outside. He listened to them talking for a few minutes, Marcy weeping and Patricia speaking softly, trying her best to console the frightened woman.

Finally Fernando got tired of standing around, so he walked through the campground to see what he could see. The tent circle was nearly full, with colorful tents erected on all but one of the tent pads. On the outer drive, where RVs were required to set up camp, most of the sites were still empty. He could see a line of RVs waiting to enter the campground, with Betty and Chet working together now to register the vehicles as they entered one at a time.

By the time he returned to Marcy's tent he found Patricia waiting for him outside at the picnic table. She looked worried. "It was our friend Earl," she said.

He nodded, not surprised.

"Marcy said he came back this morning for another so-called 'session' and she made the mistake of mentioning the digging and asking why he was interested. She said he became angry when he heard this and beat her up. Then he pushed her down on the mattress and raped her from behind. She's bleeding from every orifice. He must have been brutal. I did what I could, but I'm not a nurse—or even a medic."

Fernando nodded. "She needs to go to Urgent Care in Aztec. They'll help her report it to the sheriff's office."

"That's what I told her, but she doesn't think anyone will believe her because she's a 'sex therapist.'"

"Is she really a sex therapist?"

Patricia shrugged. "Don't know, but given her sexual antics here, she's probably right, nobody would believe her."

They stepped inside the spacious tent, where Marcy was drying her eyes with a towel and trying to compose herself. She grimaced when she caught sight of him and burst into tears again.

"The worst thing about it," she said, sniffling, "was that I kinda liked this guy. My luck, huh?"

"So it was Earl who did this to you?" Fernando asked. "The same guy who was here before?"

Marcy nodded.

"Is there anything else can you tell us about this guy? Did you notice anything you haven't told us?"

"Yeah, he has a big cock!" Marcy said, attempting to laugh.

He smiled. Patricia did not.

"But no, not really. He's short and stocky, with ratty brown hair and a ratty brown moustache. Not much of a looker. I don't know what I saw in him, to tell you the truth. I thought I could teach him a few things, but he was too impatient. He just wanted to fuck and take off."

"Was he still driving the red Ford pickup?"

"I think so."

He looked around. "By the way, why are your friends, the Bryans, leaving? They nearly ran us over on their way out. Seemed to be in a big hurry. Did they have anything to do with this episode with Earl?"

"No, they'd planned to go back to Santa Fe today. They need to get back to their shop. I'm here alone now. That's my blue Subaru."

"I'll come with you if you want company on the way to Urgent Care," Patricia said. "Or Betty Madsen, if you feel more comfortable with her. You shouldn't be alone."

Shaking her head, Marcy said, "I'll think about it."

When they left a few minutes later they again encouraged Marcy to drive up to Aztec to get medical attention and report the assault, even though it was clear she wasn't interested. So they hurried back to the camp entrance intending to help Betty, but the traffic jam had already ended. The line of cars had all but disappeared. Everyone wanting entrance to the park had received their permits and their campground registration.

Betty looked exhausted, so Patricia remained behind to help out while he went on to the visitor center, which Chet had now opened. The closed sign on the front door was gone, and several autos were parked out front belonging to visitors who were either in the gift shop or the museum.

"Do you need any help?" Fernando asked, walking up to the front counter.

"Not really, it's starting to calm down now. It's usually pretty quiet by this time of day. Most people arrive in the morning or early afternoon so they can make a day of it."

"Suit yourself."

"Oh, and Leroy called from UNM Hospital in Albuquerque," Chet said. "They have Jim stabilized. He's apparently sitting up and talking a little now. No broken bones, just a lot of bruises and lacerations. He should pull through fine, according to the doctors."

"Good news," he said.

"Someone from the FBI office is bringing Leroy back. He should be here tomorrow afternoon."

"Good. We'll need him."

Fernando went back out to the parking lot and climbed into the cruiser, but before leaving he lowered the front windows and sat behind the wheel considering his next move. There was really nothing to do until tonight. He nixed the idea of going back to Highway 550 to look for Earl, a waste of time.

Instead, he pulled out of the parking lot and drove slowly around the Chaco Loop, checking all the parking lots for Earl's red Ford pickup, just in case Earl had decided to stick around and do a little hiking or sightseeing. That seemed unlikely, but you could never tell. Like him, Earl was probably waiting around for nightfall, waiting for the action to resume.

He'd driven past the first two ruins and was in the process of driving through the Pueblo Bonito Parking lot, when he caught a glimpse of a red vehicle leaving the Casa Rinconada parking lot on the other side of the loop. He stopped along the side of the road and took a better look. The vehicle, a red pickup, was speeding east on the loop heading for the park exit. He reacted quickly, gunning the big engine and squealing out onto the hot blacktop, rippled by heat waves.

He might be able to catch the pickup if he could get to the other side of the loop quickly.

He thanked his lucky stars that no other vehicles were on the road at the moment. He slid around the curve, braking at the last minute, and then shot across the bridge over Chaco Wash to the south side of the loop. For a while he kept up with the pickup, but when the truck turned right and sped up the road out of the canyon it disappeared from his sight.

He followed as fast as he dared, bouncing over the exposed rocks and deep ruts in the rough gravel road. He cursed the cruiser, which just didn't have the suspension for roads like this. He regretted not taking the staff jeep, what a damned fool he had been. He might have been able to keep up with the pickup if he'd taken the jeep.

By the time he crested the wall of the canyon, the red pickup was nowhere to be seen. Discouraged, he slowed down and pulled off the road onto what looked like a side road or maybe a trail of some sort, just a ribbon of sand that branched out in three directions. Navajo roads or animal trails for those who lived on the plateau, he guessed. He could see two hogans in the distance and a scattering of goats foraging on the weeds and cheat grass, but no trace of the red pickup.

He scanned the horizon in every direction looking for a telltale cloud of dust, something. But there was nothing. The pickup had disappeared into thin air—or down one of the winding trails that crisscrossed the mesa, over and around a series of rocky ridges and buttes that receded into the distant horizon. He was sure of only one thing: whoever drove that pickup had a detailed knowledge of the trails on the Navajo Reservation. It was either a Navajo or someone who worked on one of the oil rigs that circled the reservation, someone like Earl.

For the hell of it, he decided to take the middle fork and see where it led. He was surprised when he found the trail flatter and less rough than the road. He followed the winding dirt trail over a ridge and stopped. From the ridge he could see great distances: the Chuska Mountains to the west, and the lofty San Juan Mountains to the northeast. Closer in he saw several hogans sprinkled across the vast desert terrain, the round Navajo dwellings that were everywhere on the reservation.

But he did not see the red pickup, so after a few minutes he turned around and started back toward the road.

Just as he reached the bottom of the ridge he came upon a small herd of goats crossing the trail, blocking his way. He stopped, watching the goats cross the trail one by one. Each of them paused in the middle of the trail long enough to turn and stare at him for a moment and then move on. He thought of honking the horn but decided against it, since he was on reservation land. In the end it took several minutes for all of the goats to get across the trail and allow him to proceed.

So out of options, he returned to the main road and drove back into the canyon, stopping at the visitor center to check with Chet. The visitor center was empty except for one young woman looking at books in the gift shop, the early afternoon rush of visitors having thinned out hours earlier. By this time of day everyone had gotten settled in the campground or were already hiking the trails they'd come to hike. Chet waved him over to the counter.

"More good news," Chet told him. "Leroy called again. Jim's up and walking around. He wants to be released tomorrow, but the doctors haven't made a decision yet. You know how hyper Jim is...he won't sit still for a moment. The man is a live wire!"

Fernando laughed. "Yeah, I can't think of anyone else who's that energetic. Actually, it's kind of annoying."

Chet nodded. "Really. Makes the rest of us look like a bunch of slackers or something!"

Fernando headed for the door, wanting to take a nap before the night watch began. It was going to be a long night, because they would be watching Pueblo Bonito as long as it took.

No more waiting.

"Oh, I forgot," Chet said, bringing him back to the counter. "The autopsy report on Pete Chavez is finished. Shows the cause of death was a broken neck, not the facial injuries."

Fernando did not respond. Turning away, he remembered seeing Tom Flynn lying dead on the floor of his home in Santa Fe with his head nearly twisted off his neck. Whoever killed Tom Flynn and Pete Chavez was strong enough to snap a man's spine like a pencil. Not a pleasant thought.

He drove back to the staff barracks, entered Jim's unit, and lay down on the sagging sofa, telling himself he had time for a couple hours of sleep before they all planned to meet for a light, late dinner. He ended up tossing and turning for two hours, tormented by nightmarish images of heads twisted off necks like bottle caps. Images followed by memories of when he was a kid watching his tiâ Maria killing chickens by twisting their heads and breaking their necks. Then she would hold the chickens down on a massive tree stump in their yard on Acequia Madre and whack off their heads with a hatchet. The frenzied, dying chickens would run madly around the yard until all their blood drained from their bodies and they simply dropped over twitching, stone cold dead. He remembered that old stump, drenched in years of dried blood that turned finally to the color of black tar, black as the night and sometimes when it rained, which wasn't that often in Santa Fe except during the monsoon months of June and July, as sticky as black tar.

Suddenly a loud pounding on the door woke him, jolting him out of his nightmares. It turned out Chet had been sent to get him, since he hadn't shown up at Betty's unit at the appointed hour for dinner. Chet joked about bringing him to the last supper. Not what he wanted to hear.

A quick sandwich and a stiff drink was all the needed to brace himself for the night watch.

"Lead the way," Fernando said.

17

It had taken some time, but Fernando and Patricia had found the perfect spot to observe Pueblo Bonito without themselves being seen. They parked on the wide gravel walkway on the east side of Pueblo del Arroyo, where they had a clear view of Bonito, about a hundred yards east of them in the waning moonlight. They'd set up about ten o'clock, deciding to take two-hour shifts. One of them would watch while the other slept, or tried to sleep as much as possible in the cramped seat of the staff jeep, which they had borrowed for the night. He went first, and then Patricia relieved him at midnight. When there was still no sight of looters at two o'clock Fernando took over.

By two-thirty a.m. he was beginning to worry that no one would show and the sleepless night would turn out to be another wild goose chase. But shortly after he took the night binoculars and began monitoring the old wagon road coming into the canyon from the west he heard the faint sound of a motor. The sound grew louder as he listened, but there were no headlights visible, just the sound of a motorized vehicle approaching slowly. Somewhere near Kin Kletso the vehicle stopped and the engine died with a last gasp.

Now he saw the silhouette: an ATV, just as he expected. He watched closely as two men jumped off the vehicle and looked around to see if the coast was clear. They put on dim headband lights and walked around behind the vehicle and removed shovels from the rear toolbox. He went to wake Patricia, but she said, "I see them. I'm wide awake now."

They watched the two men walk toward Bonito, closer to North Mesa than they had dug before. They stopped to discuss where exactly to dig and then moved a few paces to one side. Behind the partial wall of the ruin their lights were partly obscured by the jagged shapes, creating an eerie light show that reminded him of a scene from a science fiction movie that featured the lights of UFOs and aliens landing behind a stand of trees. Now the lights moved up and down as the two men began digging, up and down, like an oil rig.

"You ready?" Patricia asked.

"No, let's wait a few minutes. Let's give them enough time to hang themselves. The more they dig up, the more evidence we have. Daybreak is still almost four hours away."

Patricia agreed.

So they waited, watching the two men stop repeatedly to sort through the earth they were turning over. Eventually one of them made a trip to the ATV, carrying a small wooden crate that seemed to be empty by the way he held it with one hand. He deposited the crate in the rear toolbox and then returned to his digging, bringing with him a pickaxe and what looked like a sledgehammer. They continued digging until just before daybreak, when the sky began to lighten over the eastern wall of the canyon with a smudge of daylight.

It was then that he and Patricia decided to move.

"Now!" Fernando said.

He started the jeep and shot out from behind Pueblo del Arroyo. The jeep slid across the gravel path to the road, where its wheels caught and then, squealing, raced down to the end of the road. Sideswiping the pedestrian gate, the jeep smashed through a thick clump of sagebrush and roared up to the ATV, blocking its path and boxing it in against the Kin Kletso ruin.

They could see the two men clearly now. One was short with huge shoulders and looked like a professional wrestler or weight lifter. That would be Earl, no doubt. The other was a young Navajo, a teenager who Earl must have paid to help him with the dirty work. Maybe the same accomplice who'd led them on a wild goose chase up South Mesa the night of the fire in Casa Rinconada. Wearing camouflage pants and dark T-shirts, the two of them looked like some sort of rural militia. They had stopped digging now, looking up at the jeep and their blocked ATV, trying to decide what to do next, run or fight.

He and Patricia moved carefully along North Mesa, guns drawn. As they did the Navajo kid saw them and took off running, plunging down into the wash and disappearing into the willows and saltbush. They could hear him running on the sandy bottom of the arroyo, heading west toward the confluence of the washes and the Navajo Reservation beyond. He ran fast like a professional marathon runner who could run forever.

"Shit!" Patricia said. "I'll follow him, you take care of Earl." With that, she ran off down the wagon road in an attempt to head off the teenager before he could reach the old Highway 57 ramp, which would take him up to the reservation.

Earl, on the other hand, wasn't going anywhere. Earl waited while he approached, standing in a shallow trench with shovel in hand, ready. But ready for what? That was the question.

"Stay where you are! You're under arrest for digging in a National Park and violating the Antiquities Act," Fernando shouted.

Earl smiled, pretending to be amused by this turn of events.

Suddenly Fernando noticed the name on the stocky man's baseball cap. He'd seen that name before: Four Corners Enterprises. Now he remembered. He'd seen it on a notice at Clint Jackson's guesthouse in Santa Fe, the notice informing Jackson his application for disability had been rejected. So Earl and Clint Jackson knew each other, because they'd worked for the same company. Now, finally, he was beginning to put the pieces together.

"So you and Clint Jackson are in cahoots."

Earl's smiled faded.

Just then something caught his eye in Pueblo Bonito. It was a shadow, a black shadow moving from one fractured room to the next, just visible in the half-light of dawn. It was the same shadow of a man wearing a wide-brimmed hat and a duster that he'd seen earlier. For a split second he was startled, not knowing who or what was haunting the ruin.

That split second was all Earl needed. He brought the shovel up quickly, tossing a spade full of dirt in Fernando's face. The dirt stung like hell and momentarily blinded him.

Taken by surprise and trying to rub the dirt out of his eyes, Fernando panicked and fired off a shot in the direction of Earl. The crack of the pistol echoed off the cliff behind Bonito.

Blinking rapidly, trying to see, Fernando expected to be clobbered by a shovel at any second. Instead, he heard footsteps moving away from him and then caught brief glimpses of Earl running to his ATV—like an old movie, one frame at a time. Earl was making a run.

Though the ATV was squeezed between their jeep and Kin Kletso, Earl didn't let that slow him down. He quickly climbed aboard and fired the engine of the ATV and began smashing repeatedly into the crumbling ruin. The wall eventually fractured into a shower of rock fragments and sand, providing just enough room for the ATV to free itself and take off fast down the old wagon road, heading west toward the Navajo Reservation and the oil and fracking companies along Highway 550, including Four Corners Enterprises.

Still blinking, Fernando hurried over to the jeep and doused his face in water, drying his eyes with his shirtsleeve. Then he drove off after the ATV. It was light enough now to see the road clearly and the cloud of dust raised by the speeding ATV. Bouncing over the rough road, he tried to dodge the deeper ruts. He was glad he'd taken the jeep instead of the cruiser, which would have been useless on this road.

Once around the box canyon and past Casa Chiquita the road straitened out and headed directly for the confluence. Up ahead he saw Patricia standing beside the road with her hands raised in an attempt to flag him down. He stomped on the brake hard and the jeep skidded to a stop a few feet from Patricia, who jumped out of the way and landed on her side.

"I lost him," she said, climbing into the jeep. "He runs like a deer. Too fast for me."

The dust cloud was now far ahead of them as they resumed the chase. It disappeared altogether at the confluence, where the ATV turned north and headed toward the reservation. Fernando feared he would lose contact and so he pushed up his speed as much as he could and still keep the jeep on the road. Patricia was looking at him wide-eyed as they bounced over the rough terrain.

When the road seemed to end in a dead end, he turned due north and began the climb up North Mesa, still looking to reestablish contact. They were careening over the rough mesa now, without the advantage of a road, hoping they wouldn't hit a rock and bust the axle or the oil pan underneath.

"Over there," Patricia said, pointing to a brown cloud of dust east of them. Earl was heading in the direction of Nageezi.

So he turned sharply and raced to the east. Cresting a small hill he plunged through a stand of chamisa bush and into a small herd of goats. The goats froze, staring at the speeding jeep. One goat in the path of the jeep tried to scamper out of the way but was too slow. The jeep's right fender clipped the goat and sent the animal flying off to the side where it landed in a pile of mangled flesh and broken legs.

When he turned his attention away from the goat he saw an arroyo directly ahead of them. From a distance the arroyo looked shallow with a flat, sandy bottom. He decided to gun the motor and try to run the arroyo, but at the last second he saw he had miscalculated:

the arroyo was deep with a rocky bottom. He tried his best to stop, stomping on the brake, but it was too late to stop now and if he tried to turn sharply the jeep would overturn.

The moment before impact seemed to last forever, an eternity. Then they hit bottom, crashing into the rocks at the bottom of the arroyo and sending them thrashing about in the front seat of the jeep against the windshield and each other and into a long silence.

Fernando regained consciousness slowly and found himself in a world of pain. His shoulder felt broken or separated, and the lower half of his body was trapped under the steering wheel, leaving him to figure out how he'd managed to twist his body into this position. Patricia had been ejected from the jeep on impact and was now trying to get to her hands and knees out in the arroyo. She was clearly dazed and confused, because when she did manage to rise up, she started crawling away from the jeep going...where?

He tried to speak but nothing came out. Patricia continued to crawl away on her hands and knees.

Then he tried moving his legs, which were numb at first but slowly began to regain some feeling. He worked meticulously to extricate himself from his entrapment, one inch at a time. His survival instinct kicking in, he grabbed hold of the steering wheel and managed to pull himself up into a sitting position, ignoring the pain in his shoulder and legs. He knew he needed to be ready to defend himself if Earl were to suddenly re-appear.

Patricia continued to crawl away from the jeep, as if she had an actual destination in mind.

His spirits sank when he saw that Earl's dust cloud had changed directions and was now heading back toward them. He reached for his holster but found it empty. He looked around the front of the jeep but didn't see his Smith & Wesson. It must have ended up in the back seat of the jeep. Patricia's gun was lying in the sand only a few feet away from her, but she was moving farther and farther away. He shouted at her to stop and pick up the gun, but his shout came out as a whisper. He tried again. This time it was audible, but barely. Still, she seemed to hear him now, stopping and looking back at him, remembering. Then she looked over at the gun lying in the sand, so close but so far away.

Too late. The ATV was closing in on them fast. When it came within a hundred yards or so it started to slow down, approaching cautiously. But when Earl came close enough to see their condition–him stuck behind the steering wheel and Patricia sprawled in the arroyo–he parked his ATV and walked toward them without fear, not bothering to grab a shovel or another tool he could use as a weapon. Earl's hands would be his weapon.

Earl's smile turned into a sneer now that he had the upper hand. He came swaggering up to the jeep, looked at Fernando and then at Patricia crawling on all fours in the arroyo.

"Well, well, I'll be go to hell," Earl said. "Doesn't look like you'll be arresting anyone today, old man."

"Don't make it worse for yourself," Fernando croaked weakly. His chest hurt like hell when he tried to speak. He wondered if he had broken a rib or punctured a lung. Maybe both.

Earl laughed in his face.

"If you help us, I can put in a good word for you with the feds."

Still laughing, Earl reached out and put his hands on the doorframe, muscles bulging in his arms and shoulders. "Will you now? I just bet you would, you and your partner there." He motioned in the general direction of Patricia, who was crawling slowly but surely toward her gun.

With that, Earl reached into the jeep with one hand and tried to grab Fernando by the scruff of his neck. But he ducked and then lunged into the passenger seat, just out of Earl's reach.

"So you still got some fight left in you, eh buddy? Well, you're just prolonging your pain." Earl grabbed his left arm with both hands and braced himself to pull.

Before he could, Patricia managed to pick up her gun and squeeze off a shot, which pinged against the front of the jeep. Earl jumped back, taken by surprise. Patricia squeezed off another round, this one ricocheting off the bumper into the side of the arroyo.

Now Earl was worried. He ducked down out of sight and waited, considering his options. Crouching, he eased around the front of the jeep, calculating the distance to Patricia, who was looking around wildly, still confused. When Earl jumped out from behind the jeep, he came at her so fast she had no time to react. He kicked the gun out of her hand and then kicked her in the face, sending her sprawling in the sand with her face bloodied. Patricia screamed as she thrashed about in the sand, rolling over, trying to crawl away.

"Leave her alone, you fucking coward!" Fernando croaked.

Ignoring him, Earl kicked at the gun, then changed his mind and picked it up. "So you think you're gonna shoot me?"

Fernando watched helplessly as Earl put the gun to her head. Before shooting, he brought his hand all the way back and then smashed the pistol across her face, breaking her cheekbone and sending her sprawling in the sand.

Then Earl pointed the gun at her head.

Suddenly a loud shot rang out: Not a pistol, but a high-powered rifle. One shot.

Earl didn't know what hit him. The force of the bullet knocked him off his feet and flat on his back. His legs twitched for a few moments and his left arm came up slowly as if reaching out for a helping hand. None came. Then the hand fell back down and he lay motionless on the sand, a huge red stain spreading out in the center of his T-shirt.

Fernando waited for what would happen next. He couldn't move or turn his head to see who had shot Earl. Had Leroy made it back from the hospital in Albuquerque and come looking for them? He remembered Jim saying the rangers had one rifle they'd used to kill a rabid elk. Maybe Leroy had shot Earl with that rifle.

Or, worse case scenario, maybe it was another looter wanting the operation all to himself who would now come up and finish what Earl had started. His sense of relief faded as he realized they could still be in danger from the unknown shooter.

He heard a motorized vehicle approaching.

Patricia was weeping in the arroyo, wiping the blood from her face with the back of her hand and her shirtsleeve. She was spitting blood and mumbling something either to herself or to him, he didn't know which.

"You okay?" Fernando heard from somewhere behind them. He thought he recognized the voice but wasn't sure until he saw their Navajo friend, Ben Yazzie, approaching the arroyo. He remembered Yazzie as the man they had met on their last foray out here who had warned them about hippies and looters invading the park and trashing the reservation. Yazzie had watched events unfold from his hogan on the ridge behind them. Now he climbed down into the arroyo, looking from him to Patricia.

"Looks like you both could use some help," Yazzie said. "I told you to stay away from these people. I've seen this guy before. He pays Navajo kids to do things for him. He's a bad man."

Fernando held on to the steering wheel as if for life support. He was too shocked to speak.

Yazzie looked them over again before deciding who needed help first. He chose Patricia, grabbing a thermos of water and a roll of paper towels from the ATV. Then he hurried over to Patricia, who was mumbling to herself and trying to get to her feet.

"Careful. Let me help you," Yazzie said.

Yazzie ripped off a string of paper towels and soaked them in water and helped Patricia wash the blood off her face and hands. Then he prepared a thick pad of paper towels, soaked it in water, and handed it to Patricia to use as a cold compress on her bruised cheek.

"Wait right here."

Leaving Patricia, Yazzie came over to the jeep and forcefully pulled open the driver's side door.

"Can you walk?" he asked, offering his hand.

"Don't know," was all Fernando could think to say.

With Yazzie's help, Fernando squeezed out from behind the steering wheel and managed to turn toward the open door. He placed one and then two legs on the ground and tried to take a step on his own. Yazzie grabbed him as he fell forward and then held him under the shoulders as he helped him over to the bank of the arroyo and sat him down in the warm sand.

Then Yazzie returned to Patricia. She waited until he gave her a helping hand up and then let him help her over to where Fernando was sitting on the bank of the arroyo.

When they were settled, Yazzie went to get the thermos of water and helped them drink.

"Yeah, I've been watching this guy," Yazzie said. "He's been coming here at night. Sometimes he's with another guy. They're bad men!"

"You saved our lives," Fernando said. He suddenly felt sick, nauseated. He started to retch in the sand.

Patricia said nothing. She was sitting straight up with her legs crossed, like the Buddha. When she finally spoke, she said, "You shot him like Chis-Chilling Begay shot Wetherill. You shot Wetherill."

Part Three: Santa Fe

18

Fernando sat on a chair in an emergency room cubicle at the University of New Mexico Hospital. He had refused to get up on the table. He'd been here since noon. It took them four hours to get him into a cubicle, another hour to send him to radiology, and now a half hour to be given his prescriptions and discharge papers. Earlier some nurse trainee had brought a wheelchair to escort him to the front door but he had no intention of getting into a damned wheelchair.

The place was a madhouse, much worse than the last time he went to the Christus Saint Vincent emergency room in Santa Fe after Jimmy Mackey got drunk at El Farol on Canyon Road and started shooting up the street, him included. He liked Jimmy, except when Jimmy got drunk he saw people he didn't like, either his brother or his ex-wife mostly, and started shooting up everything in sight. Jimmy was a mean drunk and a hard man to arrest.

"Stop shooting, you crazy bastard!" he'd shouted at Jimmy out front of El Farol.

"I hate you!" Jimmy shouted.

"I'm not your fucking brother!" Fernando said, trying to wrestle the pistol out of Jimmy's hands when the gun exploded and blew off the tip of his little finger, after which Jimmy went to the drunk tank and he went to the ER. He'd spent nearly as much time in the ER as Jimmy had in the drunk tank. Bad memories....

Too much waiting, too much time on his hands, and this is what happens: the mind regurgitates memories from the past, most of them unpleasant. Where was the goddamn nurse with the goddamn discharge papers? He had been ready to leave since radiology gave him the good news that his aching rib was cracked but not broken. He was just going to be sore as hell for good long while. That was the doctor's official diagnosis: sore as hell for a good long while.

Bored, he limped down the corridor to Patricia's cubicle. She was on the bed with an IV in her arm and a cold press on her badly swollen face. "How are you doing? Can I get you anything?"

She looked at him without moving her head. "You can get me a new face. I feel like a Mack truck ran over me."

He laughed. "You look like it too."

Patricia winced, trying to laugh in spite of the pain. "Thanks. You're not looking so good yourself."

"Nothing broken, only bruises. I'm just waiting for my walking papers and opioids," he joked. He looked at her swollen face. "What are they telling you about your face?"

"They say I need surgery," Patricia said. "They're waiting for an OR now. Probably happen sometime this evening, hopefully sooner than later. What they do is make an incision in your temple and maybe put a plate and screws in your cheekbone to hold it together. Problem is, the bone takes at least six weeks to heal, so they have to give you antibiotics to prevent infection. Six weeks. That's a long time to spend recovering."

"So then you'll take it easy for six weeks? Take a break from work and go fishing?"

"Hah, I don't fish! But yeah, a long break. I think I'll go back to Crownpoint for a while. Be with my people. I know a healer who might be able to help, Navajo medicine."

"Well, good luck with that," he said, seeing a nurse coming toward his cubicle. He paused. "And thank you, you saved my life."

"And Ben Yazzie saved mine. It was a chain of events meant to be."

"You know...I think you might be right."

He squeezed her hand and went to join the nurse who was waiting for him in his cubicle. He signed on the dotted line, picked up his papers, and bid goodbye to the emergency room.

"Sir...sir!" the nurse trainee called after him, chasing him with the wheelchair as far as the door and then giving up.

At least he could still outrun a wheelchair!

Leroy was patiently waiting for him in the adjoining waiting room, where he'd been all afternoon. Leroy had no more than made it back to Chaco last night, when early this morning he had to turn around and drive him and Patricia back to Albuquerque in the Santa Fe Police Department's cruiser. He was becoming a one-man Chaco escort service!

He and Patricia both owed their lives to Ben Yazzie. After the shooting Yazzie helped them to his ATV and then took them to the visitor center, where Chet nearly came unglued when he first saw them hobble in with Yazzie's help. Chet wanted to call for the UNM medevac again, but Patricia objected, saying they would rather go by car, the same SFPD cruiser that had brought them here. Actually, he would have preferred a thirty-minute helicopter ride to the hospital, but Patricia seemed uncomfortable with that idea. He suspected she had some sort of fear of the unwieldy contraptions. At any rate the matter was decided when Leroy offered to drive them. They left Chaco shortly after nine, arriving at the emergency room a few minutes before noon. By the time they arrived the place was already packed to the rafters with sick and injured patients.

Leroy didn't seem to mind driving back and forth, though. He was always good-natured, never complaining about what he was asked to do. Now Leroy grinned when he saw Fernando limping down the hallway into the waiting room and pointed to the seats in the rear of the room, where none other than Jim Murphy waved at them. Jim had been discharged earlier that afternoon and looked a lot better than he did the last time Fernando had seen him. When they loaded him onto the medevac back at Rabbit Run Jim looked like the walking dead, as the young hiker described him.

"Damn!" Jim said, shaking his hand, "I think we've changed places, Fernando. You look worse than I do now!"

Fernando laughed so hard his ribs hurt like hell. "Not only me, Patricia's back in the ER waiting for surgery."

"I know, I saw her earlier this afternoon," Jim said. "Nasty wound. From what they tell me, though, it sounds like you got your man, one of them anyway. This Earl fellow."

"Yeah, we got the guy who was doing the digging, anyway," Fernando said. "That is, Ben Yazzie did. You heard what happened, right?"

Jim nodded. "You saved my life, you and Patricia. I never thought I'd make it out of that ruin alive. They jumped me right after my bicycle crashed in the Pueblo Bonito parking lot, two of them. Must have been Earl and the Navajo kid Patricia told me about. They took me to an old abandoned trailer somewhere on North Mesa and beat the hell out of me. That's the last thing I remember until waking up in the Rabbit Run ruin with my hands and feet taped together."

"What caused you to crash in the parking lot?"

"Good question. I really can't explain it. I saw a shadow ahead of me as I rode into the parking lot. Looked like the shadow of a man, a large man wearing a hat and cloak. Then my front tire hit something and I fell off the bicycle and hit my head on the pavement. Took me a while to get my wits back. The next thing I knew these two thugs were grabbing me and taping my hands behind my back. They kicked me a few times to shut me up and then carried me to their ATV and drove me to the trailer. That's all I remember."

"A shadow?"

"I don't know how else to explain it. It looked like a shadow or a hologram, except then I crashed into it...or something."

"Hey, let's get out of here," Leroy interrupted. "You guys can swap war stories on our way to Santa Fe."

They laughed and followed Leroy out of the emergency room, all of them glad to be leaving the hospital.

When they stepped outside into the parking lot Fernando suddenly stopped. "Wait a minute. What's the plan? Who's driving who where? And how are you guys going to get back to Chaco?"

The two rangers looked at each other. "Well, the plan's complicated," Leroy said. "We're hitchhiking, sort of. I'll drive to Santa Fe. When we get to Santa Fe, I'll stop at the National Park Service office on Old Santa Fe Trail and turn the car over to you, if you feel up to driving yourself home. And as for us, we're gonna hitch a ride on a Park Service van that's scheduled to go from Santa Fe to Farmington tonight. They can drop us off at Chaco."

"And then, hopefully, we can stay put at Chaco for a while and do our jobs," Jim added. "After all this digging nonsense, it's time for us to get back to what we're supposed to be doing: keeping the park open...and safe!"

Fernando couldn't remember where they'd parked the cruiser, but Leroy managed to find it. He was glad Leroy was driving because he was still not at full strength, not by a long shot. He hadn't eaten or slept in so long that he was feeling weak and light-headed. He needed a good meal and an equally good night's sleep. He would still be sore as hell, but he could live with that as long as he had his energy back.

Fernando rode shotgun. Jim climbed in back and then they were off on I-25 heading north to Santa Fe. It seemed like he'd been away from Santa Fe for a month—from his office at the Washington Avenue station and from his home on Acequia Madre. No doubt about it, both his boss and his wife would be mad as hell at him. He hadn't kept them informed. Chief Stuart was pissed that he'd spent so much time at Chaco and had too little to show for it. Estelle was pissed that he hadn't called every night, as was their agreement.

Once on the highway he started to relax. His eyelids grew heavy, but every time he closed his eyes he saw Earl reaching inside the window of the jeep to snap his neck like a chicken. He would have been a dead man if Patricia hadn't fired off those two shots, just as Patricia would have been dead if Ben Yazzie hadn't fired his one true shot striking Earl directly in the heart. Maybe it was all a chain meant to be, as Patricia had said.

More bad dreams. That was all he needed. Working as a detective at the Santa Fe Police Department had already given him thirty years of bad dreams, he didn't need any more.

He dozed on and off until the motion of the car slowing down woke him. They were approaching Santa Fe. Leroy turned off on the Old Santa Fe Trail exit and drove down the twisting road lined with ancient adobes on either side. The sight of the familiar adobes, their doors and windows painted bright blue and their gardens abloom with white, red, and yellow hollyhocks lifted his spirits. He loved Santa Fe, which had been his family's home for generations.

When Leroy pulled into the National Park Service parking lot he cut the engine and turned to Fernando. "Can you take it from here, or do you want me to drive you home? We could ask your wife to bring us back here, or maybe call a taxi. It's up to you. How do you feel?"

"I can drive," Fernando said. "I'm feeling better now, I think I just need some rest and something to eat."

Leroy gave Fernando a pat on the back as both of them stepped out of the car. After Fernando climbed into the driver's seat, Jim came over and poked his head inside the car door.

"So tell me the honest truth," Jim whispered, "did you see Wetherill's ghost last night?"

He looked Jim in the eye. "No," he lied.

"Well…maybe I imagined it," Jim said.

"Maybe."

19

Estelle greeted Fernando exactly as he knew she would. She said, "Why didn't you call, I've been worried sick!" And then she gave him a big hug. They were still affectionate after all these years of marriage, inseparable really, except when he had to work. They had come a long way together, he and Estelle. They were just kids when they married: he a young twenty and Estelle all of nineteen.

For the first few years of their marriage he worked part-time at Johnson's Lumber Yard and took classes at UNM, majoring in Criminal Justice. When Flavia was born, their first child, he dropped out of UNM and entered the Santa Fe Police Academy. Not only did he need a full-time job to support the family, he decided that instead of studying Criminal Justice he would rather work in the field.

Those early years in the SFPD were the hardest because of the way he and the other young Chicanos were treated. But he had a mortgage to pay and a family to raise, so he stuck it out and tried not to let the insults bother him even though they did. He internalized his anger and used it as motivation. He endured, rising through the ranks until he reached his current position as senior detective.

Early on Estelle feared for his safety every day when he left for the station, but over the years she seemed to accept the risks involved. She knew he was a careful, conscientious man who did not like to take chances. She learned to trust him, and he in turn learned to accommodate her need to be kept informed about his whereabouts and his safety. He tried to accommodate her need, anyway.

He held her at arms length and admired her petite, youthful look. Not even her streaked gray hair could diminish the fact that she had aged much better than he had. His colleagues at the station often commented on his wrinkled face, as wrinkled as a saguaro cactus was the standing joke. Too much sun, too many worries. Estelle on the other hand had few wrinkles on her face, being someone who was careful to avoid too much sun and who used sunscreen religiously.

True, he was careless about the little things like sunscreen, he just never seemed to have the time to worry about such trivial matters. Instead, he worried about the big things—like stress, for example, which was inescapable in his profession.

Estelle had dinner waiting inside, a welcome home dinner of his favorite meal: red chile cheese enchiladas with posole. He always felt a sense of relief when he stepped inside their small adobe, where they had lived since they were first married. Stress from work seemed to melt away the instant he walked into the snug, comfortable spaces of their home. The house might be small by today's standards, but it had been big enough to raise two children back in his day, before the rich Anglos from New York and Los Angeles moved into Santa Fe and remodeled the old adobes on streets like Acequia Madre into ten and twenty room mansions.

Fernando took great pride in the fact that he had preserved the original look of his simple adobe, built in the 1920s. He couldn't care less that their house had become something of an eyesore to the Sotheby crowd. Anyway, the crumbling adobe wall around their house and back patio prevented the nouveau Santa Feans from bothering them.

Estelle loved the color blue, so they had painted their front door and windows blue, which according to tradition kept evil from entering the house. Not stopping there, Estelle had hand painted their kitchen cupboards the same turquoise blue color. So far it had worked like a charm. He didn't really consider himself a superstitious man, but then again he didn't really disbelieve in superstitions either. Many of them were traditions that ran deep in the culture, so deep they were a part of everyday life, a part of who they were, call them what you will.

Over dinner he recounted what had happened at Chaco, sparing no detail, large or small, except for his near demise at the hands of Earl. He didn't want her to know about that. When he first mentioned Patricia, Estelle's eyebrows perked up, but then she clucked her tongue when she learned about Patricia's injury and the surgery she'd needed as a consequence.

What interested her most was his allusion to Wetherill's ghost, that black figure wearing a duster and wide-brimmed hat he had glimpsed out of the corner of his eye. Was it really Wetherill's ghost? He didn't know, only that he'd seen something, or someone, moving from room to room in the Pueblo Bonito ruin. No one would ever convince him that he had not seen something at Bonito.

"What about this Earl person?" she asked. "Was he acting alone or maybe with Luis Lujan?"

"Not alone. We don't know all that much about Earl yet. The San Juan Sheriff's office in Aztec is supposed to be investigating. We should know more about him soon...and who he was working with."

"What about Luis?"

He nodded. "He has to be involved somehow. He knows Tom Flynn and Clint Jackson, and he was caught red-handed at Chaco."

Estelle clucked her tongue, as she did whenever she disapproved of something, which was often.

After dinner Fernando did the dishes, as was their routine. Then they made tea and went out on the back patio to enjoy the warm evening, with fireflies in the cottonwoods along the acequia and a waning moon above in the night sky. The smell of a Santa Fe summer was in the air tonight, that whiff of sage and piñon and ponderosa pine that he so loved. Not many people knew that Santa Fe was located at an altitude of 7,200 feet above sea level, so there was always that sweet scent of mountain pine in the air, mixed with the desert flora.

After they came inside, Estelle went to their living room, where she liked to watch a little TV or listen to KUNM before bedtime. He retreated to his study to reflect on the day's events and to plan a course of action for tomorrow. He needed to have another talk with Clint Jackson. Question was, should he call on Jackson in his guesthouse on East Alameda or bring him in to the station for questioning. He decided he would have better results if he visited Jackson on his own turf. Maybe the old crank would be less hostile at home, more willing to talk freely.

In particular, Fernando wanted to know what had become of the artifacts looted by Earl. The San Juan County Sheriff had found only a few broken pieces of pottery when he raided Earl's trailer yesterday, according to Mary Alvarez, a dispatcher from the Aztec office. He'd begun to doubt that any of Wetherill's artifacts had been uncovered and to wonder if the hidden cache was a fiction. Chances were that Clint Jackson could provide some answers, since he and Earl knew each other and were clearly working together. But he was too tired to worry about that at the moment. He needed a good night's sleep.

He cringed when he stood up from his desk and hobbled down the hallway. Estelle spied him from the living room.

"You're limping! Are you hurt?"

"It's nothing," he said. "I'm just a little stiff from sitting." He hated to worry Estelle.

When she came to bed a few minutes later he was already falling into a deep, troubled sleep. He dreamed again of Earl's face suddenly appearing in the open window of the jeep and his hand reaching in to grab him, coming closer and closer. He heard Patricia scream out in pain and the crack of a high-powered rifle. And then in the darkness he saw a shadowy figure wearing a duster and a wide-brimmed hat lurking in a desolate landscape of ruins. The dark figure began to move, gliding among the fractured stone walls until it stopped and turned toward him, revealing empty eye sockets and a hollow mouth that opened wide as if to speak....

He woke up covered with sweat. He fought his way out of the wet sheet and sat for a moment on the side of the bed, trying to stop the pounding of his heart. He was afraid to lie back down.

As a last resort, he went into the bathroom and swallowed a sleeping pill. He hated taking sleeping pills, because they made his head feel fuzzy the next day, but he was desperate tonight. He needed to sleep. More than anything else right now he needed to sleep.

The last thing he remembered was Estelle moving over in the bed to make room for him. Half asleep, she muttered something unintelligible just as darkness swallowed him.

20

Someone was shaking Fernando by his sore shoulder, sending a jolt of pain through the circuits of his nervous system. He rolled over on his stomach, not wanting to be bothered. He was too deep under water to understand the voice of the siren seducing him to the surface. Closer now, he could no longer resist, fighting his way to consciousness. "Fernando, Fernando, they're calling for you," Estelle was saying. She stood over him, peering down at him as though he had been sick for a very long time. Her face came into focus slowly.

"What? Who?" he mumbled.

"Linda down at the station. The Chief wants to talk to you."

The sleeping pill had done its work. His brain felt as fuzzy as cotton, with every thought shrouded in layers of fog. Not the best way to start a day, but out of a sense of duty he struggled to a sitting position, rested for a moment, and then climbed out of bed. He walked carefully to the phone, unsteady on his feet. If the Chief wanted to talk to him, then either something big had transpired or the Chief was really pissed at him. Or both. Otherwise, he would have had Linda relay a message.

"Hold for the Chief," Linda said when he picked up the phone.

Moments later he heard Chief Stuart's gravely voice. "Lopez! Are you coming in today or what? We need you here!"

"Yeah?" Fernando grumbled, feeling the familiar tension in the pit of his stomach. Stuart had the manners of an axe murderer.

"Yeah what?"

"I'm on my way," Fernando said, a slight exaggeration under the circumstances.

"Good! It's about time you got back to work!" Stuart barked. "But listen, I want you to stop first on East Alameda. There's been another homicide in that same neighborhood, not far from the Flynn house. What the hell's going on up there, anyway? That's supposed to be one of the safest neighborhoods in Santa Fe! It has the lowest crime rate in the city!"

"Okay, I'll find out." He grabbed a pen and jotted down the street address Stuart gave him.

"Then I want you to give me a full report. I want to know if—and how—all this relates to the murders in Chaco. You understand? Between here and Chaco we have four homicides now, four fucking homicides, so what's going on?"

"Two homicides, maybe three," Fernando corrected him.

"What?"

"Two homicides that we know of, Tom Flynn and Pete Chavez," he said. "Three if this latest killing is connected. Earl Simmons was not exactly a homicide. Well, he was, but there were extenuating circumstances that—"

"What the hell are you talking about? I don't give a damn about extenuating circumstances! What's the connection here? I want some goddam answers, do you understand?"

"I'll do my best," Fernando said and slammed down the phone before Stuart could start blaming him for the lack of results.

Fernando regretted the bad blood between him and the Chief. They seemed unable to get along. To Stuart, he was a Chicano with an attitude problem. To him, Stuart was an arrogant Anglo newcomer who had no understanding of the cultural conflict that had defined Santa Fe for the past four hundred years.

Still, the Chief was right about the Chaco investigation. It was time to start connecting the dots. This was turning out to be a busy summer for homicides in upscale, usually serene Santa Fe. The fact that two homicides had occurred on East Alameda Street in the same week was downright shocking.

He ate a quick breakfast and drank two cups of coffee and then drove off in the cruiser, which he needed to return today anyway. He took the Paseo down to East Alameda and turned right, looking for the address the Chief had given him. When he passed the Flynn house he slowed down to a crawl. His spirits sank when he saw a gray Subaru Outback with bullet holes in the windows and a tiny woman standing beside the car weeping. He recognized both the car and the woman from afar: Luis Lujan's mother, Maria Lujan.

For a moment he considered driving on by without stopping. He could ask Manny or another of the detectives to take this case. Seeing Maria in the street weeping, he knew immediately who the victim was.

Not that he was surprised, given the epidemic of homicides among those involved in the plot to find Wetherill's artifacts. He just dreaded facing Maria Lujan, feeling that he should have been able to do more to prevent this latest tragedy.

Then he remembered his instructions, and once again a sense of duty overrode his desire to run. So against his better judgment, he pulled over in front of the car, which looked even older than the last time he had seen it thanks to the person who had detailed it with bullet holes in its front fender and side windows. Nothing like a few bullet holes to make a car look used.

Maria looked away, as though embarrassed, when he got out of the cruiser and walked over to the Subaru.

Inside the Subaru he saw a pool of blood on the front seat and blood splattered everywhere on the passenger's side of the front cabin. The holes in the fender were large enough to be nine mm. From the perpendicular angle of entry, it was apparent the assailant had opened fire from alongside the Outback, either on foot or in a vehicle. Given the scattering of bullet holes, the shooter must have been a piss poor shot. He guessed the victim knew the assailant, given the geometry of the shooting and the proximity of the shooter to the victim.

"My sweet Luis!" Maria wailed, coming over to him and hugging him tight. She sobbed on his shoulder, while he awkwardly patted her on the back, not knowing what the decorum was in a situation like this. He had never been good at consolation, especially in moments of crisis.

One of his weak points.

One of many, he supposed.

"I warned him to stay away from them, because these are bad men," Maria cried softly on his shoulder. "He never listen to me. He was too young and hot headed for his own good. I try to get him to work or go to school, but he never listen. He always want money, more and more money, but never to work for it, that's what I told him. And look what happen now!"

Fernando held her at arm's length. "Stay away from whom? What men are you talking about?"

"Mr. Clint. He's not a good man. I told Luis to stay away from him."

"What was he doing for Mr. Clint?"

"Running errands mostly," she said. "Picking up things for him. Driving him places. Sometimes Luis did not come home all night. I try to tell him, but he no listen to me, never."

"Were you here when the shooting occurred? Can you tell me what you saw?"

"Nothing, I saw nothing. We were in the back yard working in the garden when Luis said he had to go do some errands for Mr. Clint. He left, and the next thing I knew I hear gunshots outside. When I run out here I found him bleeding. I called nine-one-one but they said it was too late. They said he died in the car, like that. I don't know what to do now. I don't know what to do."

"Do you have anyone you could call? A relative?"

She nodded. "My sister Delores lives on Agua Fria Street, but I hate to call her, she have her own problems."

"Let me call her," he said. "I'll explain what happened."

With that, Fernando helped her inside and then called the sister and told her what had transpired and that Luis was dead. The sister said she would come right over.

When Delores arrived, he waited until they were seated in the kitchen, with Delores comforting Maria. Maria was weeping again, telling Delores what had happened and how she missed Luis.

He excused himself and went back outside to take another look at the Outback. Earlier he'd noticed the Subaru's hatch door had been popped open but hadn't had time to check it out. What he found should not have surprised him, but it did. The rear compartment was empty except for an empty wooden crate. It looked like the same crate he'd seen in the Subaru when they found Luis hiding behind the maintenance shed at Chaco Canyon.

Only a few broken shards remained in the crate. Curiously, some of the larger pottery shards had ben tossed on the pavement, as if whoever had popped the trunk was not terribly happy with what he found inside. On the pavement he saw large fragments of a bowl and a ladle, but they were only fragments and would be worth little or nothing on the underground market for Anasazi pots.

Maybe he'd been too easy on Luis, thinking he hadn't been involved in the looting. Maybe that wound on his forehead really was from Tom Flynn's cane. And maybe those broken pots were why Luis was killed: for not delivering the priceless artifacts he was expected to deliver. Maybe all he brought back from Chaco were a few shards of broken pots.

He inspected the inside of the car, careful to avoid the blood splattered everywhere. The only thing of interest he found was a pistol in the glove compartment, a new Glock, fully loaded. This was another indication that Luis knew his assailant. Otherwise he would have reached for the Glock to protect himself. If this reasoning were correct, the identity of the assailant wasn't much of a mystery.

Maria and Delores were still seated at the kitchen table when he went back into the house. "Sorry to bother you, Mrs. Lujan, but I need to ask you a few more questions."

She looked up at him.

"Do you know what Luis was transporting for Clint Jackson?" Fernando asked. "There's a crate in the rear of his Subaru with pottery shards inside. What was in the crate that he was transporting?"

"All I know is that he brought me a present a few days ago. He didn't say where he got it." She dabbed at her eyes with a handkerchief.

"A Present? What kind of present?"

"Let me show you," she said, getting out of her chair and leading him to a back bedroom. She pointed to a small bowl on a table next to a corner fireplace that was missing its bottom and a good part of its rim.

He walked over to get a closer look. He couldn't claim to be an expert on Anasazi pots, but to him the bowl looked like a classic Chaco black-on-white bowl decorated by lines and zigzags and a black ring around its fractured rim. He could tell the bowl had been recently uncovered because a layer of dirt still clung to its sides. Maybe this one broken bowl was all Earl and Luis had to show for all their trouble, all the dead bodies.

Fernando smiled at Maria. "It's beautiful."

She nodded, wringing her hands while she watched him.

"Did he bring back any others? For Clint Jackson?"

"Not that I know of. If he did, he didn't show them to me."

"Okay. Can I take a look at Luis' room before I go? I'm looking for anything that might be a clue to whoever killed him."

She led him back down the hallway to Luis' room and left him there, returning to the kitchen. He stepped inside the dark room, its windows and curtains closed tight. He found a light switch and turned on the overhead light. The single bulb cast a weak yellow glow on what looked like the room of a typical young man. Lots of electronics, including a laptop and a stereo system. A bookshelf filled mostly with CDs. Some raunchy posters taped to the wall. Nothing out of the ordinary.

Inside the closet, though, he found several boxes of ammunition pushed back out of sight on the top shelf. Behind the boxes he found extra clips for the Glock.

He closed the closet door and searched Luis' desk and chest of drawers. He even looked under the bed, finding nothing of interest anywhere.

Out of patience, he went back to the kitchen to see if there was anything else he could do for Maria before he left. This time he found her on the phone, telling the same sad story to another friend or relative.

Delores stared at him, as if he were somehow responsible for this tragedy.

"Please tell Maria to call me if I can do anything," he said and handed Delores one of his cards.

She held the card in both hands, not knowing what to do with it. "Thank you," she said finally.

When he was finished inside the house, Fernando drove back down Alameda to the Paseo and then around to Washington Avenue. He returned the cruiser to the station vehicle lot, ignoring the young attendant who made some crack about the condition of the cruiser and its thick coat of white Chaco dust that someone, probably him, would have to take to the car wash. He resisted the urge to give the young man a lesson in manners. When he walked into the Washington Avenue station he found Antonio talking to Linda at the font desk.

"Long time no see, amigo. Where you been?" Antonio asked.

"Chaco, remember," Fernando said. "Everyone seems to think I was on vacation or something."

Antonio and Linda laughed.

"Oh, by the way, whenever you're finished with your vacation, the Chief wants to see you," Linda said.

"Fuck off, both of you!"

Back in his office he reflected on this new development and what it meant for the investigation. He needed to get a handle on this before it spun out of control. Three or four homicides, depending on how you defined homicide, in less than a week and no arrests would not go over well at City Hall. The mayor and city council had a habit of coming unglued when anything untoward happened in their quiet, affluent city, anything that would damage its image as a prime destination for wealthy tourists, not to mention its real estate market! Four homicides in one week would send them over the edge. Heads would roll.

So, preparing for the worst, he took the small notebook out of his shirt pocket and reviewed his notes for a few quiet moments and then walked down the hall to face the guillotine.

21

When Fernando walked into Chief Stuart's office he found Manny and the Chief discussing something. Manny, their youngest detective, took one look at him and excused himself, not wanting to be around for the fireworks. Manny and the other cops knew he and the Chief had a troubled history: he could be prickly, and the Chief could be petulant, a combustible mix. Manny's departure left the two of them alone, sizing each other up over the Chief's desk. Stuart sat down first, and then he followed suit.

"They tell me all these homicides are connected to that fucking Flynn journal," Stuart said, a small clean-cut man wearing wire-rimmed glasses, all of forty years old. "Is that true?"

When Fernando nodded, the Chief continued: "Well, shit, this gets worse every day! We've already had four homicides. Four homicides!" Stuart shouted.

"Three actually," he said, forcing a smile.

Stuart ignored him. "What I want to know is this: why are these fools actually killing each other over this Wetherill burial, which probably doesn't even exist? And why aren't you doing anything about it?"

He listened to Stuart's familiar rant, which he'd heard more times than he cared to remember: the mayor was pissed, the city council was pissed, the better business bureau was pissed, all of Santa Fe was pissed that nothing had been done about these four murders, Four! Why wasn't he making some arrests so he—Larry Stuart—could get these assholes off his back?

"This isn't Albuquerque or Los Angeles," Stuart concluded, "this is Santa Fe, for Christ's sake! This doesn't happen here!"

After Stuart finished, Fernando took a deep breath to calm himself. He wanted to avoid another altercation with Stuart, especially now that he was approaching retirement. Over the years he'd worked hard to come to a kind of truce with Stuart, an Anglo outsider who didn't know shit about Santa Fe and its history. He didn't want to endanger his status or his pension this late in the game. He planned to enjoy himself after he retired.

"Okay, you know about Tom Flynn's murder. You also know about the journal and the cache of artifacts supposedly hidden at Chaco Canyon. We initially questioned Clint Jackson, who lives in Flynn's guesthouse, and Luis Lujan, the son of Flynn's housekeeper. Meanwhile, one of the park rangers at Chaco was murdered, so you sent me and the FBI agent from Albuquerque to Chaco, where we got involved in the investigation there."

Here Stuart interrupted Fernando's narrative. "What investigation are you talking about?"

Fernando sighed. "Of the illegal digging and the murder of the park ranger, Pete Chavez. Soon after we arrived another ranger was assaulted and kidnapped, so we stayed to help out. We set a trap and ambushed the looters the night before last, a guy named Earl Simmons or Earl Skinner, we're still not sure which, and a Navajo teenager who worked for him."

Stuart threw open his arms, wanting more.

"Earl tried to kill us after we crashed our jeep in an arroyo while chasing him, but we got lucky," Fernando said. "A Navajo rancher happened to see all this and shot and killed Earl. I ended up in an Albuquerque emergency room before returning to Santa Fe. And then this morning Luis Lujan was found shot to death on East Alameda, a couple of blocks from the Flynn house. He had a crate with a few Chaco pottery shards in the rear of his SUV, which was popped open by the assailant, I assume."

"Okay, okay, but connect the dots, I don't have all day," Stuart growled. "How are these people connected?"

"I think Clint Jackson is the key. He and Earl were friends and co-workers at Four Corners Enterprises, an oil company operating near Chaco, before he was injured on the job. He contacted Earl when he learned about the cache of artifacts, and the two of them ransacked Tom Flynn's house looking for the journal. Then they decided to work together. Earl would do the digging, and Clint would sell the artifacts in Santa Fe. Somehow Luis got mixed up with them. He was enlisted as a driver to bring the artifacts from Chaco back to Santa Fe, maybe other places, I don't know."

"Which one of them killed Flynn?" Stuart asked.

"I don't know yet. It was one of the three."

"And Luis? Who killed Luis?"

"The only person who could have. The last of the foursome."

Stuart nodded. "What about the ranger? Who killed him?"

"That would be Earl," Fernando said. "He's a muscle man with a nasty habit of breaking necks. The ranger's neck was broken just like Flynn's, and he tried to break mine when he caught up with us in the arroyo at Chaco. He would have succeeded if it hadn't been for the FBI agent. She distracted him long enough for the Navajo rancher who lived nearby on the mesa to come to our assistance and shoot Earl dead. If it hadn't been for Ben Yazzie, I wouldn't be standing here today wrapping all this up for you nice and neat so you can take it to the mayor and city council and save the day and be a big hero. Okay?"

Stuart cracked a half-smile before he caught himself and shook his head. Just a flash, but it meant Fernando was off the hook for the moment at least.

"Well shit, it looks like I owe you an apology," Stuart said, and then partially took it back: "Sort of."

Fernando shrugged. "You're a hard man to please."

"So when are you planning to pay Clint Jackson a visit?"

"I'm on my way."

"Good!" Stuart said, standing up from his desk and ending the interview. "Just one thing, Fernando. Don't shoot the sonofabitch, okay? I don't want a third killing on East Alameda."

"The realtors might have to remove its status as the safest neighborhood in the city, eh?" Fernando remarked, not bothering to hide his sarcasm.

"Exactly!"

22

Fernando had never been worried that Clint Jackson would run. Jackson was an old alcoholic with a serious disability and no money. He was also the last man standing in this misbegotten scam, the only man left who could provide answers to the remaining questions. So he had let Clint enjoy a false sense of security while he gathered the necessary evidence. He'd followed the trail of dead bodies from Tom to Earl to Luis, trying to figure out the connections. Now only one of the plotters remained alive. It was roundup time.

First, though, he had one loose end to tie up. He needed to pay a visit to Essentia and ask the Bryans a few questions. Paul and his wife June with the blue hair had left Gallo Campground in a big hurry. Why? And what exactly did Paul mean when he said they had a private collection of old pots and rugs that were not part of the regular Essentia stock?

In addition, Paul had offered to take a photo of his aura. How could he refuse an offer to have his aura revealed in living color?

He walked out to DEAD MAN in the parking lot and took it around the Paseo to Canyon Road. He found Essentia about halfway up Canyon Road not far from the El Farol restaurant. A garish adobe painted bright pink with dark red trim, the sprawling structure had stained glass windows that reflected the sunlight and made it seem like the building was glowing from the inside like an alien flying saucer, very New Age looking.

He parked on the street and walked up a flight of steps to the red door. Most Santa Feans painted their doors and windows blue because blue was supposed to offer protection from evil spirits. He wondered what the color red was supposed to offer? A satanic pact? With that in mind, he opened the door and walked into a spacious front room splashed with color from the stained glass windows. The smell of incense gagged him.

Paul materialized out of the smoky haze. He wore chinos and a black shirt today, not the ballbuster swimming trunks he'd worn at Chaco, but his hair was still moussed to the firmness of gelatin. "Detective Lopez, you came after all. It's good to see you again."

"You rushed out of Gallo Campground so fast we never had a chance to finish our conversation."

"I know! We were afraid the guy who raped Marcy might come after us next. We tried to take Marcy to the nearest hospital or urgent care facility, but she wouldn't come with us. So we just left as fast as we could and came back to Santa Fe."

Fernando nodded. "I offered to drive her to Aztec to report the rape, but she turned me down too."

"She's a strong woman, though. She came back to work yesterday. In fact, she's with a customer now."

Paul spread his arms wide. "Follow me, I'll give you a tour of Essentia. Over here, we have a first-rate selection of sexual toys." He pointed to the shelves and cabinets on one side of the room, stocked with everything from whips and masks to dildos of every size, shape, and color. Not only dildos, but other objects in various shapes and sizes to be inserted in whatever orifices the user desired to stimulate.

Fernando marveled at the variety of sexual toys and apparatuses available. Who would have thought the sexual act would require so much gear? Essentia had a more complicated view of sex than he had.

Paul continued the tour. "Over here, on the opposite wall, we have our medicinals. Lubricants, oils and unguents to juice the body, as well as stimulants like eucalyptus and ylang ylang to juice the libido. It's all about juicing, you see. If you want top performance."

"What if you prefer bottom performance," he joked.

Paul ignored his comment and led him behind the front counter into a long hallway with a room off to either side. He turned to the left. "We call this the Red Room, it's where we do most of our sex therapy."

He looked in on a dimly lit room splashed with red light. Red wallpaper, red sheets and pillows on a king sized bed. Even the Navajo rugs on the floor were red with gray stripes.

Paul turned to the right. "On the other side of the hallway we have our massage room."

In this room he saw June, wearing shorts and a halter-top, massaging an elderly man. Her blue hair bobbed up and down as she kneaded the aging flesh. They stopped to watch her place warm stones on the man's hairy back. The old man moaned in appreciation.

Paul waved at June. June smiled and waved back.

"June is a master of all trades," Paul said. "She does massage and acupuncture, as well as yoga and meditation and the more complicated treatments involved in karmic wound and energy healing."

"So you said."

Paul walked to the end of the hallway. "Here's the office and studio where we do aura photography."

He walked into the office and looked around. "Is this where you keep your private collection of Anasazi pots?"

Paul seemed taken aback. "Well, we don't have any Anasazi pots. We do have a few early twentieth century pots from Jemez and Zuni pueblos, if you're interested. On the shelves there."

Fernando took a quick look at the pots on the shelves and then walked up to Paul, face to face.

"What happened to the pots Luis was supposed to bring you from Chaco? The Wetherill artifacts? Where are they?"

Paul stared at him, not responding.

He heard movement behind him and turned to see June coming down the hall to join them.

"Tell him, Paul. Either you tell him or I will. I want this off my chest, it was a terrible mistake."

"I'm listening," Fernando said.

"Okay." Paul rubbed his forehead, trying to gather his wits. "Okay. We agreed to sell the pots. We figured if someone was going to make money selling black market pots it might as well be us. But here's the thing. We never got any pots. They never brought us anything."

"So that's what you were doing at Chaco?"

"No, we were just camping and sightseeing. We'd never been to Chaco, and they made the place sound fabulous, so we decided to take some time off and do some hiking. You saw our Mercedes Sprinter, remember? We do a lot of camping."

"And Luis Lujan was going to bring you the pots and artifacts they found, yes?" Fernando asked.

Paul shook his head. "Not him. I know Luis. It was the old man who uses the walker. He was supposed to deliver the Wetherill pots to us here."

"Clint Jackson."

"Yes, that's him."

Fernando turned to June. "Is what your husband says true? You never received any of the artifacts?"

June nodded. "It's true, we never received anything from them. It was stupid of us to agree to sell the stuff...a terrible mistake. It was Paul's idea. I'm so sorry."

"Thanks," Paul said.

June ignored her husband. "What will you do?" she asked.

"Well, if what you say is true, you never received or tried to sell any of these artifacts, then you didn't break the law. I don't intend to do anything."

"Oh, thank God! I've been so worried!"

With that, June returned to her client in the massage room.

Paul looked relieved. "Thank you."

Fernando looked around the office, searching for any evidence of a trade in black market Indian artifacts. He saw none.

"Please, step over here. Let me show you the AuraCam six thousand," Paul said. "I'd like to photograph your aura. As a way of making up for all the trouble we've caused. Or might have caused."

Fernando walked to the other side of the office, which they used as a studio. He saw what looked like an old-fashioned box camera made of gray aluminum with a black lens and viewfinder. The camera sat on a tripod facing a black background cloth hung from the ceiling. A wooden stool had been placed in front of the black cloth. On both sides of the stool sat small tables on which he saw what looked like metal hotplates. Each of the hotplates had the image of a handprint on top. The hotplates connected to the camera by means of wires.

"Take a seat on the stool, this will only take a second."

He plopped down on the stool and looked into the lens of the camera.

"Now put your hands on the metal boxes on either side of you. Put them inside the handprints on the boxes."

He did as he was told. "What? You're photographing my aura through my hands?"

Paul laughed. "Not quite, but the hands help capture the energy field around you."

Paul quickly took the photograph. He sent the image through a wireless connection to a desktop computer across the room. Then he printed the image on a nearby printer.

"Voila!" Paul waved the print in front of him. "Just as I thought. Lots of red, meaning power and passion. Not as much green as I suspected."

Fernando studied the print, which looked to him like a big glob of red ink surrounded by smudges of green and blue bleeding into the red. Like something produced by a monkey with a paintbrush.

"What's the green and blue mean?" he asked, curious.

Paul frowned. "You don't want to know."

23

On his way to East Palace Fernando swung by the Washington Avenue station to pick up Antonio. He wanted Antonio for backup just in case Clint was more dangerous than he looked. A big ex-marine with a gruff attitude, Antonio provided enough backup by his lonesome. Few people ever attempted to mess with Antonio, and those who did lived—or didn't live—to regret their foolishness. In another line of work Antonio would have been the 'enforcer.' Sometimes he thought Antonio had missed his rightful calling, although he would never say that to Antonio. He wouldn't want to give Antonio any ideas.

"Antonio, do you remember Clint Jackson, that friendly old gent with the walker?" he asked when he found the big man in the squad room. "I'm off to pay him another visit. You game?"

"My pleasure," Antonio said. "Mean little shit. Nasty mouth. Someone I can really dislike."

"That's him."

They took his Plymouth with the unflattering message scratched on its side for all to see.

Antonio paused when he saw the side of the Plymouth. "Damn! You expect me to ride around in a car marked DEAD MAN? Why haven't you taken this piece of shit to a body shop?"

"I just got back from Chaco, amigo!"

Grumbling, Antonio climbed into the Plymouth, buckled his seat belt, and sank low in his seat, as low as a six foot seven, two hundred and eighty pound man could sink in a car seat.

They followed the Paseo around to East Alameda and turned left, driving across the bridge over the Santa Fe River and into the Flynn driveway. In only a few days time the place had taken on an abandoned look, unkempt, with weeds sprouting up in the front garden and old newspapers piled up on the porch and in the driveway.

The front door was ajar, and while they watched from the Plymouth, a gray tomcat darted out of the doorway.

He noticed the tiny one-car garage at the end of the driveway. He remembered the garage door being closed the previous times he was here, but it was now open, revealing a beat-up Ford Fiesta, just small enough to fit into the tiny structure. There was no way of knowing if the Fiesta belonged to Tom Flynn or Clint Jackson, but it most definitely had been driven recently. He decided to check the sides of the Fiesta for any blood stains.

First, he wanted to take a look at the main house where Tom Flynn had lived and died. They walked cautiously up the steps to the porch and peered inside the house, which looked even more ransacked than the last time they were there. Furniture was overturned and broken glass littered the floor, as if vandals had sacked the place looking for some place to shoot up or just raise hell.

He led the way inside, stepping over the broken objects on the floor, looking into the bedroom where the boxes of papers and notebooks now covered the floor from one end of the room to the other. The place looked like it had been abandoned months, not days ago.

"Nothing here," Fernando said.

They stepped outside on the back patio overlooking the guesthouse, which was closed up tight, front door and windows closed, shades drawn. Fernando again took the lead, walking around the guesthouse to the one-car garage at the end of the driveway.

The garage door was wide open, an invitation to enter, so they accepted the invitation and inspected the Fiesta, inside and out. The inside seemed clean, but not the outside, which was covered with dust—except for the door on the driver's side, which had recently been wiped down with a wet cloth. He could see the horizontal streaks made by the cloth as Clint had attempted to wipe away all traces of Luis Lujan's blood. He'd almost succeeded, except for a few tiny drops of dried blood on the front fender and inside the curvature of the driver's side front bumper. He thought that would be enough for the lab.

Fernando smiled. The noose was closing.

Once again Antonio allowed him to take the lead. He walked across the patio to the front door of the shuttered guesthouse and knocked. There was no answer, but they heard a shuffling sound inside, the kind of sound a walker would make, so they knew Clint was inside. He knocked again, with more force this time, but still there was no response.

He tried the door. It was locked tight, so he motioned for Antonio to break down the door. Antonio obliged, ramming the door with his huge shoulder. When that didn't work, Antonio took a step back, raised his right leg, and smashed open the door. With a loud crash, the door slammed back into the wall and shook the entire front façade of the tiny house. Through the open door the inside of the house looked exactly like he remembered it, with one exception: the bedroom door was closed, and Clint was nowhere in sight.

Antonio pointed to the bedroom door and began to move forward until he grabbed his arm and held him back.

"This one's mine," Fernando said. "It's personal."

"Be my guest."

So Antonio stayed back while Fernando moved cautiously to the bedroom door. He tried the doorknob, but the door was locked from the inside. He tried to force the door open, but what felt like a heavy gauge door bolt wouldn't budge. Apparently Mr. Clint was in no mood to receive visitors. That was too bad, because he was not about to take no for an answer.

"Clint, are you inside?" Fernando asked. "Open the door, please, this is Detective Lopez from the Santa Fe Police Department. We need to ask you some questions about Luis Lujan."

"Clint! Open the fucking door!" Antonio shouted, not having the temperament to bother with the niceties of diplomacy.

"Fuck you!" came the response from the other side of the door.

Fernando motioned for Antonio to move back away from the door. "Clint, let's talk about your predicament. We know you were working with Earl to find the Wetherill artifacts. Earl's dead now. So are Tom Flynn and Luis Lujan. You're all alone now, the last man standing. If you come out now and surrender yourself, I can help you. I can work with the district attorney to get you a better deal. I can help you, if you come out now. You have my word. What do you say?"

There was a long silence.

Then they heard a plaintive note in Clint's voice as he spoke. "All I wanted was my disability pension from Four Corners so I could have something to live on. The sonsabitches wouldn't even give me what I was owed. I busted my ass for them, working on their rigs for more than ten years until I hurt my back. I had a right to that disability. So tell me, what else was I supposed to do? If we could have found the Wetherill burial, I'd be able to live like a man."

"So the burial was real?' Fernando asked.

"Yes, I already told you."

"Then why did you kill Tom Flynn?"

"I didn't kill Tom Flynn, Earl did," Clint shot back. "You should be smart enough to figure that out, Lopez. Tom and I were drinking buddies, I had no reason to kill him. Earl, though, he was a crazy motherfucker. He thought Tom was holding out on him, that he had a map showing exactly where Wetherill buried the goods at Chaco Canyon."

"And what about Luis Lujan?" Fernando asked, interrupting Clint's tirade. "How did he get involved with all this?"

"He was the driver. He was supposed to transport what Earl found from Chaco to Santa Fe, and then deliver it to me. Earl said he would pay Luis a hundred dollars for each delivery, but Luis didn't deliver shit. I don't know what the hell he did with the stuff—sell it, stash it somewhere, who knows!"

"Is that why you killed him?"

"Fuck you!" Clint shouted, angry now.

"Because all they found was a bunch of broken pots. He had nothing to deliver, that's why he didn't bring you anything."

"Bullshit!" Clint shouted. "He was fucking me over, just like Four Corners. And all I wanted was enough to live on like any other person who works all their fucking life and ends up like this. I can't work any more, don't you understand, you fucking asshole! What am I supposed to do? How am I supposed to live? Sell trinkets on the plaza like Tom?"

"Maybe the state can help you," Fernando said, trying a different tactic. "Over half the state of New Mexico is on Medicaid, it's a known fact. The state can help you if you apply."

"I don't want Medicaid, I want my pension!"

"What I'm trying to say—"

Suddenly a loud explosion ripped through the door and ricocheted off the adobe wall behind them with a pinging sound.

He hit the floor, and Antonio jumped outside on the front porch.

"Fuck you, Lopez!" Clint screamed. "I have a Glock nine millimeter in here and three boxes of ammo. The first one of you sonsabitches to come through that door is a dead man!"

Fernando crawled on his hands and knees toward the front door. Waiting for him on the porch, Antonio gave him a hand up.

"What's that?" Antonio asked, pointing to his left arm.

Fernando felt something wet and sticky running down his hand. He looked down to find blood dripping off his hand and pooling on the concrete porch. He ripped open his shirtsleeve at the shoulder and found an ugly red hole in the soft tissue under his arm, a couple of inches from his lung. Bright red blood was oozing out of both the entry and exit wounds.

"Now he's really pissed me off," Fernando said.

24

The evening light had dimmed on East Alameda Street. By now a small crowd of onlookers had gathered in the street, watching the police action unfolding at Flynn's guesthouse. Fernando had called a SWAT team earlier, but so far he had held them back, hoping to persuade Clint to come out of the guesthouse. The SWAT team commander, Ron Perez, was getting impatient. He and his heavily armed team were gathered around their armored truck at the end of the driveway, wondering why they had been called if they weren't going to be allowed to move on the shooter. They wanted to get it over with so they could go home to their wives and kids instead of standing around in full body armor sweating and cursing him for not letting them storm the house and take out the shooter.

While they waited, a medic from the SWAT team had disinfected and bandaged his wound. When the medic placed the bandage on his arm, he clucked his tongue and said, "You're a lucky man. The bullet missed bones and organs."

"Yeah, but I'd be even luckier if the bullet had missed me altogether," Fernando responded. The medic had given him a funny look.

Now, finally, Ron Perez's patience was running out. He came up and removed his helmet. "What's the hold-up? It's time to make a decision, Fernando. You either need us or you don't."

"Okay, let me try one more time to get him out. We need his testimony, if possible."

He liked Perez, a short, athletic young man who took his job seriously and did whatever necessary to protect his men. He was a good cop, as good as they come in Santa Fe.

In the end Perez agreed to let him try one more time, but he gave him an ultimatum: make a final decision about using them, or he would call off the deployment himself.

So he and Antonio moved back onto the flat porch of the guesthouse, wanting to try one last time to bring Jackson out alive.

"How's the arm?" Antonio asked.

"It stings like hell, what do you think?"

Antonio shrugged and said, "You'll live. I've seen worse. The last time I was shot it nicked an artery in my leg."

"Okay. I don't want to hear that story again."

"I bled all over the goddamn cruiser. I wouldn't let them take me to the hospital in an ambulance."

"I remember," Fernando said. "You were quite a sight when you arrived at the emergency room, blood everywhere."

Antonio smiled, remembering.

"So...if you can pull yourself away from the fond memory of nearly bleeding to death in the Christus Saint Vincent emergency room...here's the plan," Fernando snapped. "We go in one at a time as quietly as possible. You circle to the right, and I'll circle to the left. We'll meet on either side of the bedroom door. Don't, under any circumstances, get in front of the door. He has plenty of ammo, and he'd like nothing better to shoot one or both of us. Okay?"

Antonio nodded.

He entered first, crawling on his hands and knees as quietly as possible, circling around to the left side of the bedroom door. Then Antonio did the same, moving his huge body around to the right side. When they were in place on either side of the door, weapons drawn, they listened but heard nothing inside the bedroom. Not a sound.

"You want me to break down the door?" Antonio whispered.

He shook his head.

"Clint, it's Lopez again," Fernando announced. "It's time to make a decision. You can come out now and make it easier on yourself. We'll get you something to eat and some medical help if you need it. Or you can come out the hard way. The choice is yours, but you should know there's a SWAT team waiting outside. They want to storm your bedroom and take you by force. I can't keep them away much longer. If they come in, you're a dead man. So what do you say? Will you put your weapon down and come out now?"

"Fuck you, Lopez!" came the response.

"I'll help you as much as I can," he said. "I'll talk to the district attorney on your behalf. You've given us a lot of useful information.

We'll make it as easy on you as we can. All you have to do is put down the weapon and come out. Let us help you before it's too late."

"Fuck the district attorney! Send the motherfucker in, I'll shoot him first!"

"Time's running out, Clint. You can come out and live, or stay in there and face the consequences. Once the SWAT team comes in, I can't help you."

"I got nothing to live for, so what difference does it make?" Clint shouted. "They wouldn't give me my disability pension! They ruined my health, and then the motherfuckers wouldn't even give me my pension so I could live like a man, not a dog! I'm a man, Lopez! Open the door and you'll find out what kind of man I am, you motherfucker!"

But just then a loud explosion sent splinters flying from the door. This time he and Antonio were off to the sides of the door. The bullet pinged on the adobe and ricocheted across the room.

Outside, hearing the gunshot, Perez made the decision to go. The SWAT team quickly secured the guesthouse, with two men taking positions on either side of the front door, and two men circling around behind the structure. Everyone was in place, and there was absolutely nothing he could do to get Clint out of that room alive. He knew exactly what was about to happen.

When Perez gave the signal, one of the two officers in back broke out the rear window with a night-stick and the other tossed a smoke grenade into the bedroom. Almost immediately smoke began pouring out from under the bedroom door, pooling at Fernando's feet and then slowly, gracefully spiraling toward the ceiling. He heard Clint cursing and then coughing on the other side of the door. Seconds later a gunshot rang out inside the bedroom.

"Now," Fernando said to Antonio. "Break it down now."

Antonio took a step back, raised his massive leg, and with one huge kick smashed the door off its hinges. Like glass, the door burst into pieces form the force of Antonio's kick.

Fernando entered the dark, smoky room knowing what he would find. The smoke stung his eyes and irritated his lungs. Coughing, he groped on the floor and picked up the grenade and tossed it back out of the window, waiting for the smoke to clear. The room came into focus slowly, like fog lifting on a view of the Sangre de Cristo Mountains east of the city. Through the clouds of smoke he saw the shape of a man slumped over in a chair. To make his last stand Clint had chosen to wedge a cane-back chair against the foot of his bed and face the door. The Glock had fallen on the floor beside the chair.

As Fernando stepped closer he saw the bloody face of Clint Jackson: the open wound of the mouth and the spongy red mass where the top of his skull should have been. Blood and brains were splattered across the dirty sheets on the bed behind the body, like an abstract study in red and black. It was over, finished. Just like that. In one instant, life to death.

He stood looking down at the body for several long minutes. Finally Antonio approached. "Fernando?"

"Yeah," he said, and patted Antonio on the back. "You go on. I'll stick around for forensics. Thanks."

Antonio paused, as though he wanted to say more, and then changed his mind and walked back outside.

Then Fernando noticed something in Clint's left hand. He pried open the already stiff fingers and found a piece of yellowed paper torn from a book. He unfolded the crumpled paper and found a blur of illegible words and lines drawn with rough pencil on aged paper. Though the markings were faded, he knew immediately he was looking at the missing page of the Flynn journal. So apparently directions to the Wetherill loot did exist, even if the directions were indecipherable now. And that, of course, was why the three of them had killed Flynn: to get the directions. Now everything made sense. All the pieces fit together.

He left the body as he found it, except for the still open fingers that seemed to be reaching for something just out of reach. He took the torn page of the journal with him to give to forensics.

Later, after Perez and the SWAT team had gone, he sat on the porch of the main house to wait for the forensic team. He wanted to make sure none of the curious onlookers gathered out front on East Alameda Street got close enough to disturb the scene. More and more of them were arriving as the day turned into night. He didn't mind watching over the dead. He'd done it many times. It came with the territory, he knew. And in this case it gave him time to reflect on all that had happened over the last week.

Five people had died, including the four plotters and an innocent ranger, Pete Chavez. The gang of four had been victims of their own greed.

When the forensics team arrived, Fernando was still sitting on the porch. Miguel and Teresa walked up the drive from their van and nodded when they saw him waiting for them.

"The angels of death arrive," Fernando said.

"That's us," Miguel said. "Man, how many bodies are you gonna have on this street? This is our third trip to East Alameda this week!"

"We keep you busy," he said. "There's never any shortage of bodies in this business, my friend."

"Tell me about it."

Fernando took them back to the guesthouse and opened the door, pointing to the bedroom.

"Aii! Another of those!" Teresa said. She turned to him. "Why can't they just take pills or turn on the gas, drown themselves maybe, something that's not so messy!"

He shrugged.

"Just a little gallows humor," she said.

Fernando watched as they set up and started to work. "Do you want me to hang around?" he asked.

"No, we'll take it from here," Miguel said.

So he made his way outside and down the driveway to his Plymouth, where it had been parked since early afternoon. The gawkers still remained on East Alameda Street, like vultures waiting for some juicy gossip. They stared at him when he climbed into DEAD MAN and drove slowly, carefully through the crowd of onlookers, realizing as he drove how utterly appropriate the graffiti on the Plymouth had turned out to be.

He turned left on the Paseo and drove up to Acequia Madre, heading home for the night. He would file his report tomorrow morning. What difference would a few hours make? Everyone involved in the plot was already dead.

25

Today Fernando decided to take it easy. He planned to have a leisurely breakfast with Estelle, go for a morning walk along Acequia Madre, and only then report for duty at the station. All the activity over the past week or so had drained him physically and mentally. He could use a good old-fashioned vacation. Maybe he and Estelle could run up to Aspen or over to Tucson, or maybe do what Estelle mentioned: drive to San Diego and just lay on some beach for a week or so. Thing is, he hated the beach even if it was a good place to force yourself to do nothing. What could you do on a goddamn beach except listen to the waves pound the shoreline? And anyway he didn't think he had the energy for a long road trip.

As an alternative to a road trip, Estelle suggested he go to a spa somewhere close, maybe down in Albuquerque, but he hated spas and gyms even more than he hated the beach. Who wants to watch a bunch of narcissistic males flex their muscles in a mirror, or watch a bunch of equally narcissistic females soaking in hot tubs covered with mud and cucumber slices? Not him. He was thinking of a mountain vacation where he could fish and go for short hikes through the aspen and ponderosa pine.

Maybe he would ask Antonio if he wanted to come along. He knew Antonio liked to fish. The big ex-marine lived by himself and by choice in a mountain cabin near the village of Pecos, a twenty-minute drive east of Santa Fe. Antonio had been a bachelor since his marriage ended badly many years ago. Too many issues with aggression and PTS from multiple deployments in Iraq had made domestic life difficult for Antonio. A fishing trip would be good for the both of them. Somewhere quiet and far away from the job.

After discussing vacation plans with Estelle, and coming to no mutual decision about anything, he bit the bullet and drove his

Plymouth down to the station. By now he no longer paid any attention to gawking onlookers. The parking lot was nearly full by the time he arrived, all the people with problems descending on the station hoping for relief and not really understanding that the Santa Fe Police Department, in spite of their good intentions, could not solve all their problems or provide all the relief they so desperately desired.

A curious young man with red-streaked hair wearing headphones stopped to watch him pull into his parking spot.

"Cool, I dig it," the young man said as Fernando climbed out of his car. He assumed the kid meant the Plymouth, not him.

Fernando grunted and then walked into the station.

Linda looked up from the front desk. "Glad you could make it, Fernando."

"Yeah, couldn't think of anything better to do," he said, responding in kind.

"Well, you're a popular man today," Linda said. "The *Independent* has been calling all morning. Fidel wants to interview you about what happened last night on East Alameda. Lots of rumors going around about last night's shooting and this looting business. I think he wants to do a lead story on you and make you a hero...so you can't refuse the interview. Just be sure to mention Larry Stuart. The Chief wants some of the credit too."

"Most of the credit, you mean."

Linda laughed. "You said it, I didn't. Oh, and you have a visitor, a strange woman. She's waiting in your office."

A strange woman? Weren't they all?

He couldn't imagine who it could be. Perhaps Maria Lujan, still grieving for Luis?

Fernando recognized the woman as soon as he walked down the long hallway and into his office and saw the long black hair braided down her back. Patricia Begay. She was dressed in civies today, wearing slacks and a red silk blouse, with a bright turquoise and coral necklace dangling between her breasts.

"Patricia," he said, surprised to see her in his office.

She smiled. "Thought I'd stop and say hello. I'm on my way to the hot springs at Ojo Caliente. I thought I would spend a couple of days there and then head to Crownpoint for my sabbatical. I took six weeks off to recover."

"You look much better," Fernando said, sitting down at his desk. "Your face isn't nearly as swollen."

"Yeah, they put in screws so the cheekbone would heal quicker. If you call six weeks quicker!" She laughed.

"Six weeks off sounds good to me. I'm thinking about retiring again. This time I might actually do it, who knows."

"Yeah, when I was in the hospital recovering I thought a lot about leaving the FBI and going back to the Tribal Police," she said. "Like I told you, I used to work at the Crownpoint office before I joined the Bureau. I always felt comfortable there, among my own people. But I don't know, the more I thought about it, the more I felt that I should stay in Albuquerque because I was needed there. The Bureau needs a Navajo woman is what I'm trying to say."

"They do," Fernando said, agreeing. "They need you more than you need them, absolutely."

Patricia was silent for a moment. Then she said, "I heard about what happened with Clint Jackson—the standoff and the suicide."

"Turns out he had the missing journal page all along," he said. "Apparently the Wetherill cache was real, even if they never found it, and that's why he and Earl and maybe even Luis killed Tom Flynn. To get the directions on the page before Flynn could sell it to someone else."

"And they're all dead now, all four of them," she said. "Five if you include Pete Chavez."

"That's what greed does to people. Makes people crazy."

"Anglos, anyway," Patricia said, laughing.

'What? The Navajo don't have that problem?"

"Not so much. We have other problems. Plenty of other problems."

Fernando nodded, realizing how comfortable he felt with Patricia now, especially when compared to their rocky start. He remembered their silent drive up to Chaco last week. After all they had experienced, they'd managed to work through whatever was causing the tension. They'd found common ground.

"Actually, there's something I wanted to tell you," she said after a long pause. "But first, let me ask you a question. Did you talk to Jim Murphy about what happened that night at Pueblo Bonito when he was kidnapped? He came to see me when we were in the emergency room in Albuquerque and told me the whole story. I wondered if he'd told you?

"Sort of."

"Did he tell you he saw Wetherill's ghost? That Wetherill's ghost knocked him off his bicycle, and it was only then that Earl and the other man came over to kidnap him? He said they kicked him and taped his hands behind his back and then took him to an old trailer on the reservation. I've seen that trailer, it's at a place we call Turkey Gulch because back in the day there used to be flocks of wild turkeys there. The trailer must be fifty years old at least. That's where they beat him and then took him up to Rabbit Run on North Mesa."

Fernando was silent, uncertain of how to respond.

"But it was Wetherill's ghost that crashed Jim's bicycle, that enabled Earl and the other guy to come over and grab Jim," Patricia continued. "Ironic, isn't it, that Wetherill or his ghost would end up helping the looters?"

"Unless the ghost thought Jim was one of the looters," Fernando offered.

She nodded. "Maybe."

"Or maybe the ghost was trying to warn Jim about the looters. Trying to protect him."

She shrugged. "Now...about that last night in Chaco, when we separated at Pueblo Bonito. Do you remember? The Navajo kid who was helping Earl took off running down the arroyo when we surprised them? I followed him on the old wagon road as he headed west, and you stayed at the site where they were digging to deal with Earl, remember?"

"I do. You never told me about what happened when you followed him, just that he got away."

"Right, well, there's more I probably should have told you. I just never had the chance. I mean, first we were chasing Earl and then we were injured in the accident. After that, it just never seemed like the right time. Both of us could have died in the accident. Or been killed by Earl."

"We were very lucky," Fernando said. "Thanks to you and Mr. Yazzie, we're here today."

"So here's what I want to ask you. Just when we surprised them, before the kid took off, did you see Wetherill's ghost up at Kin Kletso?"

"I saw a shadow. Something."

She nodded. "So did I. And I saw it again when I was running after the kid hoping to cut him off before he reached the old Highway

Fifty-seven entrance. I was near the box canyon, across from Casa Chiquita, when I saw the kid run out of the arroyo and make a dash for the entrance ramp. I started to go after him, and that's when I saw it, the shadow of a man wearing a cape and a big hat."

"That's near the spot where Wetherill was murdered in nineteen ten," Fernando added, more to himself than to Patricia. She knew more about Wetherill than he did.

"Exactly," she said. "He moved, or floated, out of the ruin toward me. I stopped, thinking I might be in danger. Just then the moon went behind a cloud and the canyon went dark. I lost sight of the ghost and the kid, although I could still hear the kid running up the old road over loose rocks. When the cloud passed, I saw a huge black dust devil swirling toward me on the road. I was too frightened to move or call out. I just stood there as this rotating cloud of dust engulfed me. It felt like I was being restrained by swirling winds instead of ropes. I couldn't see. I could hardly breath because the winds were so strong. The dust devil lasted maybe a minute or so before it stopped just as suddenly as it appeared. It was like someone hit a switch and the wind just stopped dead."

Fernando listened, nodding his head, trying to make sense of what he was hearing. He neither believed nor dis-believed in ghosts, but he'd lived in magical Santa Fe long enough to know there were more things in this life than could be explained by a simple rationalist philosophy. That was especially true in places like Santa Fe and Chaco Canyon, where cultures and entire civilizations were layered on top of each other, haunting each other. You couldn't walk—or dig—anywhere in this state without uncovering bones and artifacts of the ancient ones. All New Mexicans walked on haunted ground.

"What happened next?" he asked.

"When the wind stopped and the dust began to settle, I saw the ghost coming toward me again," Patricia continued. "Except this time he had his arm out, as if he were pointing at me or something beyond me. I didn't know if he meant to help or harm me. I still can't decide."

"Maybe he wanted you to help him," he said.

"Could be," she said. "He did seem to be reaching out to me, as if he wanted my help. But how could I help him?"

"Maybe by helping him keep the looters out?"

"Yeah, I thought of that, but then why would he help the kid get away? The kid was a looter. And so was Wetherill, for that matter. At least that's what most people believe today."

"Or maybe he wanted to let you know that he's still watching over the canyon," Fernando offered. "He died an angry man. Angry at the federal government in Washington for taking Pueblo Bonito away from him, angry at Edgar Hewett and the other archaeologists for ruining his reputation, and angry at Chis-Chilling-Begay and the other Navajos for murdering him. So angry he's unable to move on from the spot where he was murdered."

"An angry ghost who can't or won't move on from where he was murdered," she said slowly. "I like that. It makes sense. I think you might have some Navajo in you, Fernando."

He laughed. "Probably so. We've been mixed up together for what, four or five centuries?"

"Long enough," Patricia said. Then, after a long silence, she said, "Well, I just wanted you to know what I saw in case you have to go back to Chaco."

"I can't say I'm looking forward to going back there anytime soon," he said. "Too many ghosts, as you say."

She stood up and extended her hand. "So...I'll say a prayer for you at Ojo Caliente."

He shook her hand warmly. "Thanks, Patricia. I can use all the prayers I can get."

"Look me up if you're ever in Albuquerque...or over in Crownpoint while I'm recovering."

"How long will you be in Crownpoint?"

"I'll need another six weeks, the doctors tell me."

Fernando smiled, thinking he might just ask Estelle about taking separate vacations. She could go to the beach in San Diego with their daughters and he and Antonio could go fishing.

"Just so happens I've been think about taking a vacation. Maybe I'll go camping in the Cibola National Forest. I used to like fishing in Bluewater Lake. Haven't been there in years."

"That's not far from Crowpoint."

He handed her a yellow legal pad. "Here, write down your cellphone number."

She wrote down the number and handed back the pad.

"We made a good team," Fernando said, smiling up at her.

"Yes we did," she said. Then she turned and walked down the long hallway into the sunlight.

Readers Guide

1. At first Detective Lopez dismisses the idea that Tom Flynn was murdered to obtain a single page of a dusty old journal. What changes his mind?

2. What is the source of the friction between Detective Lopez and Chief of Police Larry Stuart? What's their history?

3. Detective Lopez is assigned to work with FBI agent Patricia Begay. When they first meet, Begay is somewhat distant, even unfriendly. Why? How do they overcome this awkwardness?

4. What is the American Antiquities Act of 1906 and what does it protect? How does it affect the course of action in Ghost Canyon?

5. FBI agent Begay resents being sent to Chaco Canyon, where she is noticeably uncomfortable. Why? What is the Navajo history with Chaco?

6. FBI agent Begay speaks repeatedly about the ghosts of Chaco Canyon. Does Detective Lopez believe in ghosts? Does his attitude change in the course of their stay at Chaco?

7. Richard Wetherill was the first amateur archaeologist to excavate ruins at Chaco Canyon. He sent an enormous quantity of Chacoan artifacts back East to those who had provided money for his expedition. How do the various characters in the story regard Wetherill?

8. The Chacoan empire lasted from about 860 to 1200 A.D. What are the standard explanations for the 'fall' of Chaco? Which of them seem more likely to you?

9. Explain the chain of events that lead Detective Lopez to believe that Earl is involved in the looting at Chaco and the murders of Tom Flynn and Pete Chavez?

10. A Navajo rancher named Yazzie rescues Detective Lopez and FBI agent Begay. In doing so Yazzie shoots and kills Earl. Why does Begay say, "You shot him like Chris-Chilling Begay shot Wetherill. You shot Wetherill."

11. At the end of the mystery Clint Jackson takes his own life rather than be arrested by the SWAT team outside his guesthouse. What does Detective Lopez find in Jackson's hand? How does that provide the final clue that explains what has transpired?

www.ingramcontent.com/pod-product-compliance
Lightning Source LLC
Chambersburg PA
CBHW010140030826
48979CB00024B/1075

* 9 7 8 1 6 3 2 9 3 4 0 7 9 *